THE WEEPING CHAIR

THE WEEPING CHAIR

DONALD WARD

thistledown press

© Donald Ward, 2012
All rights reserved

No part of this publication may be reproduced or transmitted in any form or by any means, graphic, electronic or mechanical, including photocopying, recording, or any information storage and retrieval system, without permission in writing from the publisher or a licence from The Canadian Copyright Licensing Agency (Access Copyright). For an Access Copyright licence, visit www.accesscopyright.ca or call toll free to 1-800-893-5777.

Thistledown Press Ltd.
118 - 20th Street West
Saskatoon, Saskatchewan, S7M 0W6
www.thistledownpress.com

Library and Archives Canada Cataloguing in Publication

Ward, Donald B. (Donald Bruce), 1952-
The weeping chair / Donald Ward.

Short stories.
Issued also in an electronic format.
ISBN 978-1-927068-00-7

I. Title.

PS8595.A692W44 2012   C813'.6   C2012-901125-8

Cover photo: Shutterstock Images
Cover and book design by Jackie Forrie
Printed and bound in Canada

 Canada Council for the Arts   Conseil des Arts du Canada      Canadian Heritage   Patrimoine canadien

Thistledown Press gratefully acknowledges the financial assistance of the Canada Council for the Arts, the Saskatchewan Arts Board, and the Government of Canada through the Canada Book Fund for its publishing program.

ACKNOWLEDGEMENTS

"Badger" was awarded first prize for short story in the 2009 CBC Literary Awards and was read on CBC Radio and published in *enRoute Magazine* in June 2010. I am indebted to the CBC, Air Canada, and the Canada Council for their judgement and their generosity.

Thanks to Kimmy Beach for reading earlier versions of many of these stories and offering sound advice and valued support.

Thanks to Wayne Sanderson for telling me the original story of the weeping chair.

Thanks to the baristas at Starbucks for explaining their vocabulary.

Thanks to Jared Ward for sharing his knowledge of small aircraft and the particular difficulties of — theoretically — pushing someone out the passenger side door while in flight.

Thanks to Brigid and Caitlin for being such awesome daughters.

Special thanks to my editor, Seán Virgo.

for Colleen, beloved companion of 14,000 days

Contents

11	*Things You Can Do on a Train*
29	*My Grandmother's Teeth*
38	*Father Kennedy's Jubilee*
44	*The Perfection of His Failure*
59	*Trundling through the Glen*
76	*The Sins of the Fathers*
92	*The Weeping Chair*
106	*The Accidental Whore*
113	*Asylum Chorus*
122	*The Blingt Quartet*
131	*The Ladies of His Flock*
148	*A Woman Clothed with the Sun*
172	*Life with a Hole in the Middle*
181	*Badger*
189	*The Mad King's Army*
217	*Epilogue*

Things You Can Do on a Train

I didn't like to tell him he was on the wrong train, but I didn't want him sitting next to me for three days either. He was a pale specimen, and lean, with limp hair and an uncertain complexion, probably the result of inadequate nutrition in childhood. I thought it must hurt to have so much bone, yet so little flesh to cover it. He was wearing a dark, pinstriped suit, of a good cut but shiny at elbow and knee; I had seen several like it in the Salvation Army store on *rue Notre-Dame* a couple of days earlier.

"I have to be in Calgary by Saturday," he said.

This train didn't go to Calgary.

"Faster by plane," I commented.

"Couldn't get a seat," he said. "All the flights were booked." He gazed morosely out the window as the tenements crept past. "What time does the bar car open?"

"I don't know."

He stopped a passing trainman, who affected not to understand English. They were allowed to do that between Montreal and Ottawa.

"*Le bistro,*" I intervened, for I was allowed to speak French between Montreal and Ottawa. I pointed to my watch. "*À quelle heure . . . ?*"

The trainman pulled out his pocket watch and gazed at it fiercely for a moment before rattling off a sentence in rapid

Québecois, of which I caught every second or third word. He marched down to the end of the coach before we could take up any more of his valuable time.

"What did he say?"

"He said the bar car won't open until we leave Ottawa."

"When do we get to Ottawa?"

"A couple of hours, at the earliest." I looked at my watch, as if that might speed things up. "Then we'll be at least an hour in the station."

I watched him working out the mathematics. "You mean, I won't be able to get anything to drink for three hours?"

"Probably closer to four," I said.

"But there are only two things you can do on a train: sleep and drink. Everybody knows that."

There was a third option, which I proceeded to take. He asked me what I was reading. I showed him the cover.

"What's it about?" he asked.

"It's a sequence of poems about place, time, and memory," I said. "It's about self-consciousness and transcendence. Some critics believe it's his greatest work."

"What do you do?" he asked.

I closed my *Four Quartets*, not impatiently, but trying to convey the sense that my attention would be of limited duration. I am reluctant to tell people what I do, especially people on trains, because they have so many questions to which I must answer no. No, you can't make a living at it. No, you wouldn't recognize my name. No, I don't write pornography.

"You're a poet?" He was not as surprised as I would have expected. "You make a living at that?"

"No."

"You have any books?"

"Not yet."

At his insistence, I listed a few literary journals that had published my work. He recognized none of them.

"Ever tried porn?" he suggested. "Bet you could make a killing at that."

"Yes, but there's been too much killing already."

He gave me a puzzled look, then laughed. He wasn't really interested in me.

"What do you do, Bill?" I asked, for we had exchanged names in a manly sort of way — the quick handshake, the perceptible nod — after I told him I was a poet. I expect he wanted to test my grip.

Bill gazed out the window, his eyes scanning the skyline. He was developing cataracts, I noticed. Untreated, they would eventually render him blind.

"There," he pointed.

We had passed through the inner city, and the landscape had expanded to include warehouses and docks, dark with soot and labouring men. In the middle distance, a radio transmission tower rose above the roofs. I gave Bill a questioning look.

"I build radio stations," he said.

I had a sudden image of my angular seatmate, pinstriped and wing-tipped, scrambling up the outside of a structural steel tower. I had once climbed a fire tower in Prince Albert National Park, and frankly, I couldn't see that he was fit for it.

"That's interesting," I said, and returned to my Eliot.

Bill was smoking now, du Maurier filters, which he lit with a hissing butane lighter.

"Have to be out of my apartment by Sunday," he said.

"But you have another place to move to," I told him, not looking up.

"Haven't had time to look," he said.

"Why do you have to move?" I asked. Actually, I didn't, but I knew that was the question he would answer whether I asked it or not. First he paused, looking away as he pulled on his cigarette. Then he put it out — evidently with some pain, to judge by his expression — in the ashtray in the arm of the seat.

"I've been evicted," he said, puffs of smoke escaping his lips like lost souls, punctuating the consonants.

I couldn't say I was surprised, but I raised a questioning brow.

"They're converting my building to condos," he explained, "and I refused to buy."

It was a point of principle on which he was anxious to expand. My lack of reaction seemed only to encourage him.

"Why would I buy an expensive little box downtown," he asked, bitterly, "when I could get a three-bedroom bungalow for the same price a little further out?"

"Why don't you?" I asked. "Get the bungalow, I mean."

He dismissed the suggestion with a gesture and lit another cigarette. "I like to be close to the action."

I silently added lying to the list of things you can do on a train, after sleeping, drinking, and reading. By rights, I suppose, lying should have headed the list. People who build radio stations don't buy suits from the Family Thrift Store, and they don't travel by day coach, no matter how many planes are full or how soon they have to get to Calgary. People don't wear suits on day coaches, either, unless they have nothing else to wear. I could see him fixing radios, maybe, in his pinstriped suit, poking into a cramped transistor compartment with a soldering gun as smoke curled up into his eyes. I could see him moving from one seedy hotel room to another.

"Where you headed?" he asked.

"Saskatoon."

He nodded. "I was in Regina once."

"So was I."

• Things You Can Do on a Train •

I thought we had exhausted the possibilities for conversation when a gap-toothed man in a crumpled khaki blazer lurched by, reeking of liquor and grinning like a ferret. He had a head like a serving dish, and it seemed to be serving raw beef. I had never seen someone so ugly that I wanted to hit him. He staggered forward and threw himself down three seats ahead.

"Looks like he got an early start," said Bill.

At the time, I believe, the Canadian National Railway had a rule about drunks on the train: in coach class, there had to be one in every car. There also had to be an asshole. We had found our drunk. It was only a matter of time before the asshole self-identified.

There was another rule, but it was more subtle. Whereas a third of the seats in day coach had *No Smoking/Défense de Fumer* stickers affixed to the bulkhead above the window, it was generally understood that compliance was optional. In the rest of the car, however, smoking was mandatory.

Bill put out one cigarette and lit another.

"Maybe he's got some to share," I suggested, nodding forward to where our gap-toothed friend had collapsed.

A look of hope came into Bill's clouded eyes. "Can't hurt to ask," he said.

It did hurt, as it happened, and Bill returned to his seat rubbing his hand. "Bugger bit me."

I nodded. "I was watching."

All I had seen, in fact, was Bill's long right arm reaching out stealthily, and then swiftly being withdrawn. The teeth were faster than the eye.

"Son of a bitch," said Bill, flapping his wounded hand. "You don't bite a guy just because he asks you for a drink."

No, I thought, *but maybe you bite a guy who tries to slip a hand into your inside pocket to lift your mickey while he thinks you're unconscious.* I added a fifth item — biting — to the expanding list.

The train came to a restless halt, as trains often do. Bill craned his neck to look out the window. "Now what the hell?"

"They're probably waiting for a freight train coming from the opposite direction," I said.

He sat back, rolling his eyes. His collar was riding up. "So we're supposed to sit here, twiddling our thumbs, while some freight train tries to make up for lost time?"

"When you consider that the alternative is a violent collision, with inevitable fatalities, it doesn't seem that bad," I said.

He nursed another cigarette as we waited. He loosened his tie and opened his collar. He wasn't very good at waiting. But soon enough a deep rumble in the tracks announced the approach of the expected freight train, and our coach shivered in the slipstream as it swept past. Bill relaxed visibly as our own train coaxed itself back into motion.

We pulled into Ottawa thirty minutes late, and we were another hour in the station as the dining cars were provisioned. Our gap-toothed friend rose to temporary consciousness, looking surprised, as if his presence among the living were the result of some cruel prank. He drained the last of his mickey, then produced another from one of his bulging pockets. He made substantial inroads into that one before passing out again. Bill never took his eyes off him. A few more people got on, gazing about in alarm or displeasure before choosing their seats.

A woman of singular beauty took a seat across the aisle and immediately took out a large and complicated piece of needlework, which she spread out on the seat beside her. She had flowing oak-red hair and a scattering of matching freckles across the bridge of her nose. Her intent was as clear as if she had posted guards. *Don't even think about talking to me*, it said. I could see her on a wingèd horse, conducting the slain to Valhalla.

• Things You Can Do on a Train •

    An elderly couple halfway down the car arranged to have a younger passenger moved so that they could sit together. This was not accomplished without incident, for the younger passenger wanted the space to himself. First they asked him politely, then they reasoned with him, then the woman burst into tears, then a trainman ordered the young man to another seat. An unfortunate feature of the old man was that his left earlobe was grotesquely elongated and discoloured, like a bag of smashed olives, and it flapped against his neck as he spoke. This had the effect of turning aside the sympathy of his fellow passengers, which would normally have been his without question, and we were well out of Ottawa before the matter was settled.
    "Why doesn't he have the damn thing amputated?" my seatmate asked, no doubt echoing the thoughts of his fellow travellers.
    "Maybe he's allergic to anæsthetic," I said.
    The younger passenger, on the trainman's instructions, found himself beside a plain young woman wearing a pastel pullover and Capri pants. She did not welcome her new seatmate, and clung to the window side, her purse a barrier between them.
    A middle-aged couple returning from a funeral arranged, with less fuss, to move a stout, lightly bearded woman in a print dress from one seat to another so that they might journey together. "We just buried my brother," said the man, as the displaced passenger took her place beside a stranger. Her limp smile of sympathy was not reflected in her eyes.
    We were now at full occupancy, aside from the vacant seat beside the Valkyrie across the aisle and another beneath the gap-toothed drunk, who was sprawled across two seats and looked unlikely to be moved. The conductor and a trainman made their way up the car, taking tickets and checking destinations. Bill contrived to be out of his seat when this occurred.

"I thought I saw someone in this seat," said the conductor as he checked my ticket.

"He was just visiting," I said.

"Guy in a pinstriped suit?"

"Must be from another car."

The conductor gave me a long, hard stare, which I returned without flinching. Poets are subversive by nature, and I had had experience staring down vice-principals through four years of high school. "When does the *bistro* open?"

"Any minute now," but it was a good half-hour before a porter stuck his head in and announced that the *bistro* was now open for all passengers, and Bill strode past without a word. He must have been hiding in the washroom.

He returned to his seat almost immediately.

"Buggers won't take a cheque," he complained.

"Did you expect them to?"

"Well, yeah . . ." I knew what was coming. "Would you...?"

I reached into my jacket, which was hanging on a hook against the bulkhead, and gave him a five-dollar bill. The familiar blue portrait of Sir Wilfrid Laurier disappeared with astonishing speed as Bill palmed it.

"Thanks, buddy," he said. "I'll pay you back as soon as we get to Calgary."

You're not going to Calgary, I thought, *and you know I'm not going to Calgary, either.* But I considered the five dollars a reasonable investment. I read in peace for a couple of hours while the woman across the aisle plied her needle with undivided concentration, occasionally referring to a book of patterns which she kept in a voluminous handbag at her feet.

They were working the bar in shifts, Bill explained when he returned. Patrons were allowed to stay and drink as long as there were no passengers waiting, but as soon as there was a lineup the porters would stop serving whoever had been there the longest. Bill was one of the first to be evicted.

"Ever watched a man die?" he asked, following some obscure train of thought.

"As a matter of fact, I have."

He was interested to hear it. "What happened?"

"He fell from the top of a fire tower in Prince Albert National Park."

"Bet that was ugly," he said.

"It was," I assured him.

"How'd it happen?"

"I pushed him."

"You're not serious."

I turned a page.

"You're having me on," Bill persisted, but I let him think what he wanted to think. After a moment, he said, "I was in 'Nam."

I closed my book again. "Canada wasn't in Vietnam," I informed him. "That's why so many draft dodgers and deserters sought sanctuary here."

"I didn't mind killing Commies," he went on, as if I hadn't spoken, "but when my buddy took a bullet in the chest I decided it was time to ship out." He let that sink in before adding, "He died in my arms."

"How many Commies," I asked, at length, "did you not mind killing?"

"I put a few guys away," he said. "Corporal in my unit used to cut off their ears and wear them on a string around his neck, but I never believed in taking trophies."

Neither had I, so I didn't bother calling him a liar.

"You don't believe me?" He had sensed the weight of skepticism hovering between us. "Check this out."

He hiked up one pant leg to reveal a jagged scar on his calf muscle. "That's where the bayonet went in" — he turned his leg — "and this is where it came out." There was a corresponding scar on the other side of his leg. "That's what got me out," he said. "Wounded in action. Honourable discharge."

"So what brought you to Canada?"

"Couldn't stand all the bullshit." He scowled. "They want you to kill for them and make the world safe for democracy, but they don't want you marrying their daughters, and they sure as hell don't want to hire you."

For the first time, I wondered if he might be telling the truth. For his part, he was soon wondering how he might get back into the bar car.

"Take off your jacket and vest and maybe they won't recognize you," I suggested. "The tie as well, and roll up your shirt sleeves."

I gave him another five dollars, which I could ill afford, but it bought me another few hours of reading. As the day wore on into darkness, I had a ham sandwich and coffee in the buffet car, standing up to ease the boredom of sitting. When I got back to my seat, Bill had returned, and seemed to be sleeping peacefully. Later, as the dome lights dimmed, the train stopped again. I might have caught a few moments of sleep then had it not been for the rising of a sharp, hectoring voice near the front of the car.

"It's ridiculous!" he was complaining, to no one and everyone. "We've been stopped for forty-five minutes. I'm less than an hour from my home. I can practically see the lights from here. We were supposed to be there, according to the schedule — the *printed* schedule," he emphasized, "five hours ago. I could get there faster if I got out and walked! I'm less than an hour — "

"Shaddup!" commanded a loud voice beside me, which gave me a start, for I had thought Bill was asleep.

"Did you tell me to shut up?"

"If you don't like the service," said Bill, his eyes still shut, "get out and walk."

"Well, I have an answer for you," the man said, not sure whom he was addressing. "You have your opinion and I have mine."

"Keep it to yourself."

"I probably *could* get there faster if I *did* walk!"

"Nobody's stopping you," someone else said.

"Here I am, less than an hour from my home. I can practically see the lights..."

I got up and walked to the front of the car to use the washroom. I easily identified the asshole. Discontent was plain on his mobile features — his eyes, ears, and mouth moving in rhythm to a distant but disillusioned drummer. His hair was tufted front and back, as if he had escaped before the barber was finished.

"They're waiting for the other half of the train," another passenger was explaining to him as I emerged from the washroom.

The asshole's eyebrows and upper lip rose in unison.

"Half a train leaves Montreal at ten o'clock in the morning, travelling northwest at an average speed of forty-five miles per hour through congested suburbs," the passenger was saying. "The other half of the train departs from Toronto at noon, travelling in the same direction at approximately the same speed. At what point on the north shore of Lake Superior do the two half-trains converge, and how long does it take them to become one train travelling west?"

The asshole thought about that for a moment before muttering, "Asshole."

"That role has been filled," I said, to general applause from nearby seats.

"We've been stopped here for forty-five — no, *fifty-five* — "

"Shut up," said the other passenger.

"I'm less than an hour — "

"Shut up," the other passenger repeated, this time to more sustained applause from nearby seats. Hearing so many arrayed against him, the asshole settled into a determined mutter.

As I returned to my seat, I noticed that the young man and the girl in Capri pants had reached an agreement of sorts, and were now exchanging fluids beneath a blanket. I added one more activity to the list.

"That was good," said Bill, as I resumed my seat.

"It was," I agreed.

As the train jerked into motion I composed myself for sleep, reclining my seat and folding my hands over my belly. I felt my body rocking with the movements of the train, which were neither regular nor gentle. I closed my eyes, but they kept opening.

The Valkyrie across the aisle had put her things away and was gazing into the measureless distance. Elsewhere in the car, people endured the semi-darkness in their different ways, some grunting in discomfort, some moaning, some heaving deep, repetitive sighs, a lucky few snoring. Sometimes a head popped up to look around. People visited the washrooms at either end of the car. A few who ventured onto the swaying platforms between the cars for a breath of fresh air were swiftly herded back inside by flat-capped trainmen shouting about danger and the law. Nothing draws a trainman faster than an open door and a hint of oxygen.

At some point in the night the train stopped again and the necessary asshole disembarked, wondering aloud if there was anybody waiting to meet him, or if they had sensibly gone home to await his phone call from the station, which was now closed.

Periodically, an important-looking bunch moved through the coach, followed almost immediately by an equally important-looking bunch coming back. It was the crew: four hours on, four hours off. They looked neither right nor left, and made a show of not touching the seat backs to steady themselves. Concentrating as they were on this mildly prideful exercise, they paid no attention to my sleeping seatmate. But once again, when the train stopped at a remote outpost to let passengers off and bring others on, Bill managed not to be present when the conductor came along to check our tickets.

"No one sharing this seat?" he asked.

"Guy slept there most of the night," I said, "but he was so drunk I don't think he knew where he was."

The conductor nodded grimly. It was a scenario that had played itself out relentlessly through the course of his career.

Bill reappeared in the morning, munching on a roast beef sandwich and holding a styrofoam cup of coffee. I could see the individual bones and muscles of his jaw working away as he chewed and swallowed.

"Haven't eaten since we left Montreal," he said.

I went to the dining car, where I lathered toast with honey. I don't like honey, but a vegetarian had once advised me that it would get me through the day. I was badly in need of a shower and a shave, but contented myself with the thin trickle of tap water in the washroom, where I brushed my teeth and rinsed my hands and wet my face. When I returned to my seat, Bill was opening a fresh pack of du Mauriers. He looked, not surprisingly, like a man who had slept in his suit, but I was entirely surprised when he reached into an inside pocket and produced a ten-dollar bill. Even the portrait of Sir John A. looked a little surprised, I thought, as Bill repaid his loan.

"Had a run of luck last night," was all he said. "I wonder when the bar car opens."

"It's eight o'clock in the morning, Bill."

"Hair of the dog," he replied.

The Valkyrie had her needlework out already. She seemed to be making a tapestry. I caught sight of leaves and vines and the occasional human face. Bill slept off his hangover beside me. The gap-toothed drunk, now regrettably sober, took his overnight kit into one of the washrooms and emerged twenty minutes later with bits of toilet paper clinging to his shaving wounds. Shortly after that he began to nurse his second mickey, taking short sips, trying to make it last.

The morning passed without incident. When the bar car opened I decided on a liquid lunch, based chiefly on the unexpected repayment of my ten dollars. The man with the distended earlobe came in with his wife and they had one drink each, a Bloody Mary and a gin and tonic, both poured from pre-mixed bottles. I watched the man's dangling appendage tremble with the movements of the train, and had a sudden, repellent image of his wife stroking it in privacy.

I sat with a combative girl from Vancouver who was on her way home from an educational exchange in St. Pierre and Miquelon, the tiny islands in the Gulf of St. Lawrence that represent the last remnant of the French Empire in North America. She had acquired a taste for Bordeaux, she confided, and the porter dutifully emptied one six-ounce bottle after another into her plastic glass. They spoke in French to one another, and I understood that he approved of wine and young women and hadn't asked for proof of age. She was a generous tipper.

"If I've learned anything in the past eight weeks," she declared in English, turning to me, "it's that I hate my parents."

"Seems a bit extreme," I remarked. I was drinking Molson's and the porter was being generous with the pretzels; I wouldn't have to buy another meal that day.

"I've been gone for two months," she said, "and I didn't miss them once."

I tried not to show any interest. She, in response, related her life story, which seemed mostly a tale of blight and resentment: a privileged upbringing, private schools, a generous allowance. She had a bedroom to herself on the train. But her father wouldn't buy her a car, the cheap bastard. When she spoke of her parents, her lips framed the words like a flexing noose, as if she would throttle them as their names escaped her larynx. If she hadn't missed them in these eight weeks, I thought, it was an even bet that they hadn't missed her, either.

"Necrotizing granuloma," she said.

I had not been listening closely, but those eight strange syllables brought me up. "I beg your pardon?"

"The old guy's ear," she explained, flicking her earlobe. I looked around to see if the couple had left. "It's a kind of tumour where the tissues die. My dad had a case once. He's a doctor."

When I returned to my seat, Bill was reading *Four Quartets* and frowning.

"If all time is eternally present," he said, "and all time is unredeemable, then it doesn't really matter what you do in the future, because you've already done it."

"Most people read T. S. Eliot for insight," I said, "not permission," but with four ales and half a pound of pretzels inside me, I was in no mood for a literary discussion. I thought I might just be able to catch a nap.

The Valkyrie had so far held herself aloof, but she proved no match for the gap-toothed drunk who had bitten my seatmate the day before. Fully conscious now, and desperate, he had long since finished his second mickey and was now making his way from passenger to passenger, trying to borrow money.

"I have two hundred dollars waiting for me in a bank in Winnipeg," he said, deftly avoiding the thrust of her needle as he took an uninvited seat on her tapestry. "Can you believe it?"

"I'm sure all two hundred of them are eagerly awaiting your arrival," she said. It was the first time I had heard her speak. Her voice was deep but musical, a contralto.

"I've a murdering headache, so I do," he told her, in a parody of an Irish accent, perhaps his own. "I just need a little drink to calm me nerves."

She reached into the bag at her feet and produced a bottle of Aspirin. "Take two of these," she said, "and go to bed."

"Aw, you're killing me," he said.

"No," she responded, "you're killing yourself. You don't need my help."

"Can't you just lend me a few — " but then Bill flung a long arm across the aisle and backhanded him. It was done with such economy of movement that for a moment the man didn't know what had happened. He didn't even feel the pain right away, but rolled his eyes and fell back into the seat before finally yelping like a kicked dog.

"Neatly done," I said.

"Thank you," said Bill.

Without a word, the Valkyrie rose and stepped over the drunk and made her way to the washroom at the back of the car. Bill and I were not the only men who watched her progress.

"Callipygian," I said.

"Calli-what?"

"Callipygian," I repeated. "It means pronounced or well-formed buttocks."

A trainman came by then. He gazed at gap-tooth for a moment, as if trying to reconcile the broad platter of the man's head with his own experience of self-consciousness and transcendence. Failing, he said, "You're in the wrong place, my friend. You'd better move."

"Move?" The notion was foreign to his experience.

"Back to your own seat," said the trainman, and escorted him there. "If I catch you drinking illegal alcohol on this train, you'll be put off at the next stop."

When the Valkyrie resumed her needlework a moment later, she looked across the aisle and said, simply, "Thank you."

"You're welcome," said Bill.

I must have slept then, for the next thing I was aware of was a hammering headache and a powerful thirst. The windows were black with the night, and the train was picking up speed as it cleared the boreal forest and commenced its straight run across the great plains. This was where they began to make up for lost time.

The seat beside me was vacant. I found Bill in the bar car, hiking up one pant leg in the aisle to show his scar to a couple of younger men across the table.

"... and that's where it came out," he was saying.

"Wow," said one of them.

He made room for me on the seat beside him.

"Hair of the dog," I explained, and he nodded approvingly.

"Rye and ginger," I said to the porter, who was hovering nearby.

"No, no, *no*," said Bill, shaking his head emphatically. To the porter, he said, "Straight rye, no mix."

I nodded feeble assent. When the drink arrived, I gave it a tentative sip.

"Toss it back," he urged.

I tossed it back. I felt my gorge rising. Flames came out my nostrils. It was sheer force of will that kept me from vomiting. Bill immediately ordered another, and, to my surprise, paid for it.

"He's a poet," he explained to the two young men across the booth. "Got a book coming out next year."

"Wow," said one of them. They were lumberjacks, returning west after a season in northern Ontario, pockets overflowing with cash they'd had no chance to spend in the bush. One of them bought a round for the table. "Ever tried pornography?" he asked. "Bet you could make a killing at that."

"There's been too much killing already," Bill said.

We fell into a meditative silence, swaying with the liquor and the train. At length, I turned to Bill and said, "You're not really going to Calgary, are you."

"And you didn't really throw a guy off a fire tower in Prince Albert National Park, did you."

It seemed a time for truth, so I admitted that I hadn't, "but I wrote a poem about it."

They arrested him in Winnipeg. A railway cop boarded the train with an RCMP constable, and Bill wasn't quick enough to escape. They had been tracking him for weeks as he crisscrossed the country, a thief in the night on the paths of iron.

"Are you going to write a poem about me?" was the last thing he said as they led him away.

"Human kind cannot bear very much reality," I replied.

My Grandmother's Teeth

My grandmother's voice made me think of alligators calling out to one another across a swamp. After seventy years, she no longer smoked, she just inhaled; it went in, but you never saw it come out. On a still day you could hear her breathing from any room in the house. Her accustomed chair in the family room bore the scents of her age and her addictions: tobacco, malt whisky, hand cream, urine. It was impossible to imagine another wrinkle on her face. But her teeth remained a startling white. My mother said it was because she soaked them in bleach every night, but no one knew for sure. No one in the family had ever seen her put them in or take them out, and we had no idea where she kept them when they weren't in her head. There was a story that my grandfather had once walked into the bathroom to find her scrubbing her dentures in the sink, but the tone of her voice when she demanded that he knock before entering a lady's toilet conveyed such a mixture of outrage and contempt that he resolved never to do so again. He didn't get the chance, poor man, because he died soon afterward, leaving his widow to mourn for a year before selling her house and moving in with us.

"Whatever happened to that old chair of my mother's?" my father asked one evening at the table.

"It was *not* a Stickley," my mother responded. "She bought it out of an Eaton's catalogue."

"I was only asking," my father sighed, completing the triangle of misapprehension.

It was an established pattern: one of them would ask a question, the other would respond obliquely, then the first would take offence, usually with a deliberately understated display of patience, which was inevitably — and accurately — judged unnecessary by the other, who would then retreat into a wounded silence, which would eventually erupt in anger.

Later that evening, meaning to avoid the scene, I decided to take the dog for a walk. It was a tactical error, for it meant that I had to go through the kitchen, where my mother was opening drawers and slamming them shut, to the back porch, where the dog cowered in neurotic apprehension.

"Two years," my mother was muttering. "Two years and all of a sudden he wants to know where the damn chair is. Fine for him. *He* didn't shampoo the seat once a week and then stay up half the night with a blow dryer so she'd have a dry cushion to leak into in the morning. Two years," she repeated, her voice rising as she turned to me. "I burned it. I soaked it with her last bottle of lighter fluid and set fire to it. Right there." She pointed into the darkness beyond the porch. "Wood, stuffing, petit-point cushions, and her last half-carton of Rothmans. Went up like kindling."

"I'm going to take the dog for a walk," I said.

"Fine," she said, "take the damn dog for a walk, but don't expect your grandmother's chair to be here when you get back because I *burnt it*."

"Digby," I said, for that was the dog's name, "we're going for a walk."

"Where do you think you're going?" demanded my father, who had ridden in on the crest of my mother's rant.

"I'm taking Digby for a walk."

"Not before you've done your homework." He always tried to exert a little parental authority when his marital authority was under threat. "You know the rules."

"I've done my homework," I said.

"Well, then, that's all right," he said, and as I stepped into the porch I heard him say, "Alice, why *are* you opening and closing the drawers like that?"

"I'm looking for your mother's chair," she told him.

I heard their voices rising as I clipped the lead onto Digby's collar, and then the pair of us departed into the night. Digby led me feverishly down to the end of the yard, where he waited, taking little springing steps while I opened the gate. Once we were in the alley, he had permission to relieve himself, which he proceeded to do, first on the neighbour's compost heap, then on their garbage bin, then on the fence of the neighbours across the alley, and then on *their* garbage bin. It was the dog's way of sending messages. At the same time, he collected the messages that had been left by other dogs. Dogs have twenty million sense receptors in their noses. I can only imagine the complexity of their correspondence.

People have told me that Digby is an undignified name for a Malamute, and I suppose it is, but he lived in a porch, after all. He ran from small children and edged away from dark corners. If there were a queue of faithful animals waiting to defend me, Digby would be the last in line. But my father only let me go out after dark if I took the dog with me.

People have told me that Malamutes are a short-lived breed, for their hearts can't sustain the powerful bodies that human beings have bred them into. But I suspect life seemed quite long enough for Digby. They say that Malamutes are headstrong and difficult to train. I think Digby had brain damage. Still, if it weren't for the dog, I would pretty much regret being an only child. It's true he never spoke to me, but at least he listened, and I took pleasure in the company of an animal that did not regard me as a creature to be pitied.

Digby never knew my grandmother, except by her lingering odours, for he arrived a full month after she died. My father frequently forgets this, imagining that his mother might have squeezed another year or two out of life had we not radically altered her daily routine by bringing a young and lively, demanding new creature into the house, but she was in the ground four weeks before the dog crossed the threshold. I marked it on the calendar. But my father's memory relies more on what might have happened than what did, and neither my mother nor I have ever managed to disassociate Digby's arrival from my grandmother's death.

Malamutes are a cold-weather breed, which explains why Digby lived in the porch. Most days the house was simply too hot for his comfort. Even on the coldest winter mornings I would find him curled up on his blanket, the tip of his bushy tail against his nose, the water in his dish frozen solid. As it was good for me to "take some responsibility once in a while," as my father was fond of saying, it was my job to take the dog for his morning walk and then snap the ice from his bowl and give him fresh water when we returned. That was his only sustenance until the bus brought me home at four o'clock and I gave him his daily ration of dry dog food. I often thought of my grandmother's teeth when I fed the dog, for the hard little bits of mechanically deboned beef and animal byproducts that tumbled into Digby's plastic dish had been, according to the package, "specially formulated to keep your dog's teeth clean and free of tartar." I tried to brush Digby's teeth once, but he didn't like it.

I remember the day with clarity. I had entered the house through the back porch, which was my practice long before Digby was there to greet me. I had my own key because my parents had misplaced all the others they had hidden over the years. I knew where each one was, rusting and useless, under which stone, which flowerpot, but I liked having my own key, and they eventually decided it was safer in my pocket than anywhere else, though they still insisted I come in through the back door lest the old woman across the street call the police, as she often did when she saw people letting themselves into houses at odd hours.

I turned on the radio in the kitchen and switched to the FM band. My parents, who each worked until five and rarely got home before six, had forbidden me to do this because classical music set my grandmother's teeth on edge. Instead, I was to go through to the family room and keep the old woman company until they came home. She grew lonely, they told me, once her afternoon television programs were over. In fact, she grew thirsty, and the unspoken understanding was that, during this interval, I was to monitor her intake of malt whisky and make sure she didn't burn the house down with her constant and careless smoking. In practice, I generally found her snoring in her chair, with half a dozen cigarettes burned down to the filter in the ashtray. I would take her glass away and return the bottle to the liquor cabinet, and then enjoy an hour or so of music as I cleared and washed the breakfast dishes, started supper, and did my homework at the dining room table.

When my parents came home, one of them would invariably notice that the radio was on the FM band instead of the AM they preferred, because I never remembered to switch it back. I would swear that I had not been listening to opera, which was how they defined all classical music, and then lie about my grandmother's liquor consumption. The old woman usually awoke on my parents' return and reached for her cigarettes, but she never asked me where the whisky had gone, and no one ever remarked on the regularity with which the bottle had to be replenished. For reasons that remain unclear to me, these daily deceptions were necessary to the functioning of the family.

If my father then offered his mother a glass of sherry, as he did most evenings, she would respond with a disingenuous, "William, I would *love* a glass of sherry!" as if she hadn't tasted drink for days.

"Stimulates the appetite," my father would concur, and the pair of them might go through half a bottle of Tio Pepe before my mother got the meal on the table. She liked to think she managed this without help, and became bitter when no one thanked her for it. Then she would start muttering and my grandmother would smoke another half-dozen cigarettes before wheezing off to her bedroom.

But on this day I sensed another presence in the house. It was death, but I was not to know that. I went through to the family room. The scene held no surprises — the cigarette butts, the half-empty bottle, my grandmother leaning back with her eyes closed, mouth open — except that I couldn't hear her snoring. It was a moment before I realized that she wasn't breathing at all. What finally convinced me she was dead was the fact that she wasn't wearing her teeth.

"She never goes anywhere without her teeth," my father said, on viewing the corpse. I had called him from work, and he was not pleased. "Do you know where they are?"

"No."

"Have you looked?"

I hadn't. I had assumed, naïvely, that he would be more concerned about his mother's death than the location of her teeth. When my mother arrived fifteen minutes later, she took matters in hand, calling the police, the coroner, and a priest, in that order. The police could do little but register the deadness of the body, which the coroner confirmed and the priest anointed. It was the coroner who had her packed up and taken away. The cause of

My Grandmother's Teeth

death was soon established — heart failure, which surprised no one — but it was another two days before my father found her teeth in a nineteenth-century egg coddler she had been given as a wedding present in the previous century. I remember his call to the funeral director.

"I've found my mother's teeth," he began, then: "What? Are you sure? ... Well, I suppose that's all right, then," and he hung up.

"They say she's ready for viewing," he said, baffled, holding my grandmother's teeth in one hand and gesturing helplessly with the other.

"How can she be ready for viewing without her teeth?" my mother asked.

"They say it's all been taken care of," said my father, this time gesturing with the hand that held the teeth, which grinned like some ghastly, lipless mannequin at the end of his arm.

"Put those things away, William," my mother said. "They're revolting."

I did not find them revolting so much as pathetic. My grandmother's teeth were the only things she had left that might have been seen as desirable. She had been failing in the past few months — I had noticed it, if my parents hadn't; the cigarettes and whisky were taking their toll — and it came to my mind that perhaps she had been unable to remember where she put her teeth that morning, and the indignity of it was what finally carried her off.

I did not see what my father did with them, but when we attended her funeral the following day it was clear that she was wearing someone else's. Her thin, wrinkled lips were firmly closed over a set of dentures whose previous owner had obviously taken much larger bites than my grandmother had. I assumed the mortician kept a store of them for such occasions, but he might have made a more judicious selection in this instance. My parents were so grossed out by the possibilities that they refused to discuss it. So we buried my grandmother with her lips glued shut over someone else's teeth, and the subject was closed.

It was not long afterward that I heard them discussing my future. "The boy," as they called me, should not come home to an empty house every day, and as there was now a terminal shortage of grandparents, a dog seemed the next best thing. I would rather have had a computer. My parents both had sleek little laptops that they brought home each evening and took away again in the morning, but they assumed I would be incapable of learning the use of one, so instead of a computer I got Digby, who soon became my sole responsibility. He was the runt of the litter, they said, and might have been bullied to death by his siblings if my parents hadn't stepped in.

Digby had the run of the house initially, but soon demonstrated a preference for the unheated back porch. "Out of sight, out of mind," was my parents' philosophy. I doubt it occurred to them that it was Digby's philosophy as well. When dogs look at humans, they see not a different species, but members of their own pack, to whom they must be subservient. Dogs that do not accept their place in the pecking order are apt to be abandoned by their masters and eventually euthanized at the SPCA, but most are clever enough to acknowledge this fact of life and govern their behaviour accordingly. Like a minor official in a corrupt regime, Digby made a home for himself as far from the axis of power as possible.

It was Digby who eventually turned up my grandmother's teeth. He must have found them when he still had the run of the house, and clandestinely taken them when he retired to the back porch. My grandmother was the one member of our pack he hadn't met, yet her scent remained everywhere. Perhaps the dog regarded her dentures as a sort of relic, the castings of a dead saint. I have a mental image of him playing with them, day after day, then

My Grandmother's Teeth

returning them to their hiding place when he heard me coming home. But one day he wasn't fast enough, and I opened the porch door to find him grinning like a Cheshire Cat, my grandmother's teeth in his jaws. I wondered if it was intentional, for there was something in the dog's demeanour that suggested he knew more than he was letting on.

"You stupid dog," I said, and he bobbed his head in affirmation. I took my grandmother's teeth from him, and they sat grinning at me on the dining room table as I listened to the radio and did my homework. They were no longer white and perfect, but stained and scratched, and broken where Digby had gnawed at them.

Before my parents returned home that day, I took my grandmother's teeth out to the back yard, where Digby and I buried them.

Father Kennedy's Jubilee

Julie was a well-made woman, with regular features and a figure unspoiled by childbirth or excess. Emmett loved her, but no amount of physical beauty could make up for a complete lack of interest in sex. Twice in the past year he had suggested to her that, as she didn't seem to be enjoying sex any more, they might as well abandon the activity, for it wasn't much fun for him, either. But then Julie would have another period, which meant that she was still fertile, and Father Kennedy had made clear to them the church's teachings on licit sexual relations. Childless in their late 40s, Emmett and Julie were yet bound to try, earnestly and regularly, to conceive, allowing nothing to impede the possibility, not even voluntary celibacy: they had rejected that option when they married. In the meantime, they were to pray.

Emmett thought Father Kennedy was talking through his hat, but Julie was silent on the subject. If she resented calling her uncle "Father," experience had taught her that it was easier than not. Even her father called him "Father," his own brother. Her uncle wore his dignity like a starched suit, invoking familial or sacerdotal authority as the occasion demanded. They were returning from his fiftieth anniversary mass at an obscure rural parish a hundred and fifty kilometres east of Saskatoon when a remarkable thing happened.

"I can't help but think," said Emmett, "that if I were celebrating my fiftieth anniversary of ordination, I would have found something more appropriate to preach about than obedience and birth control."

"Like what?" Julie asked.

"Oh, gratitude, grace, faith, the rewards of service."

"He was called by God," Julie reminded him. "He had no choice."

"Oh yes, he played that old saw again, but I don't suppose God called him to the imitation of Christ just so he could annoy people."

As Julie knew, her uncle's search for God had taken him to four dioceses before he finally found a bishop who was willing to "journey with him," as he put it, down the peculiar and unforgiving path God had chosen for him.

"Why do you think the bishop put him out in the middle of nowhere?" she asked.

It was a rhetorical question, but Emmett answered it anyway. "Presumably so that he could preach fidelity to the pope and imply that the victims of sexual abuse have only themselves to blame."

They were cruising at a comfortable few points below the speed limit on a long, narrow stretch of Highway 5. A low, black automobile with dark tinted windows pulled up behind them and started hugging their tail lights.

"He's always been a bully, Emmett."

"Well, he certainly managed to bully the few souls who showed up this afternoon."

"At least he thanked us for being there," Julie noted.

"The chicken was like jerky."

"You could have choked on the breast meat," Julie agreed.

"And the rest of it," said Emmett. "Jellied salads, pasta salads, everything soaked in mayonnaise, and then he had to get up and speak at that, too."

Emmett checked the speedometer and increased his speed to match the posted limit of 100.

"The man is mad."

"Who, my uncle?"

"Quite possibly," said Emmett, "but I was speaking of the driver behind us."

Julie looked in the side mirror. The car was edging up and falling back, then edging up and falling back again. "He doesn't seem to want to pass," she said.

"No," said Emmett, "he's trying to force me to go faster."

"Why would he do that?"

"Because it's not worth his while to pass someone who's only going the speed limit."

"I don't understand."

"He's an asshole," said Emmett.

"For goodness sake," said Julie, "pull over and let him pass."

"Where am I supposed to pull over?" Emmett gestured toward the shoulder of the road, which was barely wide enough for a bicycle.

"Ooooh!" said Julie as the car lurched to the left.

"You see" — Emmett put both hands back on the wheel and corrected — "he's already got me rattled."

"Slow down, Emmett."

"I can't."

"Why not?"

"He won't let me. He wants me to pull ahead, then he'll pull up again and I'll increase my speed again, and he'll pull up again. He has to make it worth the effort to pass me at 120 or 130 kilometres an hour."

"How do you know that?"

"Because I'm a man."

"That doesn't make any sense," said Julie.

"What I don't understand is, why doesn't he just retire?"
"Who?"
"Your uncle."
"Old priests don't retire, Emmett. They just grow mouldy at the altar."

Emmett put his foot to the floor. The engine, unused to such treatment, hesitated and coughed, then rose to the occasion. Julie, glancing fearfully at the dashboard, had a sudden insight into the function of a tachometer. The needle rolled wildly over the top of the gauge, kissed the redline, fell back, and then rolled over and kissed it again. She felt her body pressing into the seat, heard the whine of the cylinders as they were at last allowed to do what they had been designed for: heat, speed, quick breaths caught in the throat. Had they been travelling in a Porsche or a BMW, they would have been well beyond the limits of experience before Emmett lost his nerve and backed off. In a Jeep Cherokee they peaked at 150 kilometres an hour, then levelled off at 130, then gradually settled down to a more sedate 120. Even at that, Emmett was breathing heavily.

Julie was not breathing at all.

The black car pulled out and passed, effortlessly.

"See?" he said. "He had to have his victory, just like your uncle."

"You can hardly blame this on my uncle," said Julie.

"I wasn't, I was just — " but then a hand reached out the driver's side window of the car in front. It seemed to be holding some sort of animal.

"What the hell is that?" asked Emmett.

It was a cat, sleek and black like the car, head into the wind, ears lying back.

"He can't be doing what I think he's doing!"

Julie was appalled. Emmett honked the horn. He pulled out and tried to pass — to what purpose he didn't know, but he couldn't just do nothing as the man threw his cat out of the car. But the low, dark vehicle kept pace, matching Emmett's speed and acceleration, and in the end Emmett and Julie could only watch helplessly as the outstretched hand slowly released its grip and the cat slid from it, almost gracefully.

Julie had her iPhone out.

"What are you doing?"

"I'm calling the police."

"What are you going to tell them?"

"What do you think I'm going to tell them?" She shook the phone impatiently and tapped in the emergency code again. Cell phone reception was notoriously bad along Highway 5. "A man just threw a cat out of a car."

"While you're at it," said Emmett, "tell them that the cat is running alongside."

"Don't mock me, Emmett."

Emmett pointed. "Look for yourself."

The animal had hit the blacktop running. It fell back a few lengths, then it adjusted its stride and slowly, impossibly, began to overtake the car.

"You *do* see what I'm seeing, don't you?"

Julie leaned over for a better look. "Look at his legs move!" she said, in awe.

She had a hand on Emmett's thigh, clutching him at the horror of it, then stroking him with increasing urgency. She had a strange look in her eye.

"What a magnificent animal!"

According to Emmett's speedometer, the cat was doing 110 kilometres an hour. Its back was flexing like a beating heart, its black fur rippling, nose into the wind, a purely physical creature of muscle and grace.

"Pull out," said Julie, "so I can see better."

Emmett pulled into the oncoming lane.

"Wow," said Julie.

It was impossible, of course. Some explanation would occur to them once the surprise and excitement was over. Yet Emmett got a sense almost of pleasure emanating from the animal.

God made me small, it seemed to be saying, *but he also made me fast.*

As they watched, the driver's tinted window rolled down. A hand came out and the cat jumped into it. The hand withdrew. The window rolled up, and the car sped away as if the Jeep had been standing still. Emmett lurched back into his lane.

Julie was still stroking his thigh. Emmett was not an intuitive man, but he sensed there was something on her mind other than cats.

"What did you say?"

"I said there's a side road half a kilometre ahead."

Emmett pulled over. There wasn't another car in sight. Not that it mattered. The world could have been watching and they wouldn't have cared.

The Perfection of His Failure

"That is the deadest priest I have ever seen," the bishop remarked.

"We did our best," said Gosling the funeral director, quick to perceive a slight where none had been intended.

"Yes, well, I think we'll have a closed coffin for the funeral."

"But all my work — "

" — was not enough," the bishop interrupted, "to make the poor man look as if he had merely fallen asleep."

The figure in the coffin looked like a wax impression that had begun to melt. The lips, uncharacteristically but firmly shut — by what art the bishop dared not guess — had retreated slackly down his cheeks, so that instead of a mouth the corpse now had a four-inch slit disappearing at either end into shallow folds of doughy flesh. The eyelids, too, succumbing to gravity, had begun to sag toward his temples. The hands folded across his jacket, a rosary entwined in the fingers, looked like slabs of pork lately taken from the fridge — and were nearly as cold, the bishop reflected, for he had touched the dead flesh as he blessed it.

"A closed coffin," he repeated. "No point in alarming people unnecessarily."

Gosling made no attempt to hide his displeasure. The expensive chemicals, the wax, the make-up, the hair gel, the hours spent trying to *un*murder this corpulent cleric — all for naught. A closed coffin, indeed. What was the world coming to?

"God will reward you," said the bishop, "and so will the diocese. Submit your invoice and it will be honoured. Thirty days net," he added.

"If you will not reconsider — "

"I will not."

" — then I might as well seal the casket now."

"Just make sure it's sealed when you bring him to the funeral mass."

The mortician was a rigid, unlovely man who bore a striking resemblance to the late V.I. Lenin, bald of head and sharp of beard. But whereas Lenin the despot had spent his energies slaughtering the innocent and the ungrateful, Gosling the undertaker had chosen the gentler art of making them look alive again, if not awake. He was capable of genuine concern when a grieving spouse chose to honour a lost partner appropriately, but there was no joy to be got from these priests. Might as well put the bugger in a packing crate and be done with it.

"He lived a life of consecrated poverty," said the bishop, reading the thoughts in Gosling's face. "He owned nothing and would have had no wish to be displayed in mock splendour after his death."

Gosling gave a shallow bow that managed to convey more of contempt than respect, and walked away.

Inspector Harriet Linden was waiting for the bishop in a room off the chapel — not the generic, non-denominational chapel at the funeral home, but the chapel of St. John Chrysostom College, where the bishop had lately been reading the Office for the Dead with the late Father Sylvester's confrères.

"What do I call you?" was the first thing she wanted to know.

"Brendan will do."

"Ah . . . I'm afraid I can't."

"Bishop Rush, then," said the bishop, settling his bulk into one of the two metal chairs that faced each other across a low table. "And you?"

"Harriet Linden," said Harriet. "Inspector Harriet Linden."

"I'm pleased to meet you, Inspector Linden."

Harriet doubted it. She took a digital recorder from her purse and placed it on the table. "Do you mind?"

"As a matter of fact, I do. This is a reconciliation room."

"A what?"

"A confessional, if you prefer. We have long since emerged from the darkened closet where the penitent knelt on one side while the priest sat on the other, but we still respect the seal of silence." He pointed to the recorder. "It would set a dangerous precedent."

"This is not a formal interrogation, Bishop Rush, I just — "

"I'm pleased to hear it."

Harriet did not like being interrupted, especially by a bishop. A celibate by circumstance, she distrusted those who were celibate by choice. The bishop, for his part, admired the long legs in their flesh-hugging pants that proceeded from Inspector Linden's bountiful hips, which were amply visible in the too-small chair. He enjoyed being a man, never more so than in the presence of a beautiful woman, and Inspector Linden was certainly that. Her brief, functional hairstyle and the severely practical rimless spectacles she wore were entirely inadequate to disguise a face so regular in feature and pure in expression that Bernini might have sculpted it in marble. *A strong woman*, he thought. *A woman of determined principles. A woman,* he thought, *who would shake a rat by the neck until it died.* He thanked God he was allowed to look, but no more.

Harriet was aware of the bishop's eyes on her. She had been led to believe that many priests of the Catholic Church were gay. Brendan Rush was clearly not one of them.

"This is not a formal interrogation," she repeated, "but simply a request for information. We know the circumstances of your colleague's death, but — "

"He was stabbed through the heart," the bishop interrupted again, "with a thin, double-edged blade, a stiletto." He mimed the action in the space between them. "I can imagine a pimp carrying such a weapon, can't you?"

"Do you know many pimps, Bishop Rush?"

"Very few."

"Then kindly allow me to proceed at my own pace and in the direction I choose to go."

She has the rat by the neck already, thought the bishop, and nodded for her to proceed.

"As I was saying, we know the circumstances of your colleague's death, but very little of the circumstances of his life. What can you tell me about your Father Sylvester?"

"In the first place, he was not *my* Father Sylvester. He belonged to the order that administers this college. He took vows of poverty, chastity, and obedience, but his obedience was not to me; it was to his superior-general in New Mexico, which is the seat of his order. In theory, the bishop is in charge of the diocese, but I can't always be aware of what one canonical superior or another might be getting up to behind my back."

Harriet had been frowning.

"You're not Catholic," the bishop intuited.

"In English, please, Bishop Rush."

The bishop leaned back in his chair, which had been designed for a penitent. The back was too low, the seat too short, and the combination was beginning to torment him.

"Perhaps," he said, "we might continue this interview in my office at the cathedral rectory, where we can sit in chairs that were designed for human beings and sip tea or coffee if the urge overwhelms us."

Harriet smiled without humour. She was not going to let him gain the advantage so easily. She knew the rules. She had bent them often and skillfully enough that she wasn't about to take any crap from a highly placed cleric.

"I'd rather continue here and now," she said.

"Alas," said the bishop, "the choice is not yours," and he raised his bulk from the mean little chair and proceeded to vacate the room.

"The thing is," he continued later, in his office, "Father Sylvester's situation was anything but clear. His order had all but expelled him. They could command his obedience, but not his conscience, and in the end they could not even command his obedience without denying a fundamental truth of the Gospel. Instead, they followed the time-honoured ecclesiastical practice of setting him adrift."

"Bishop Rush," said Harriet, impatiently. She was smarting from having been outmanoeuvred at the college. "What I need is intelligible background information. Who was Father Sylvester? Where did he come from? What was his function in the diocese? And why would anyone want to stab him with a stiletto?"

The bishop sat back in his cushioned office chair. "I'll do my best, Inspector. But I must warn you that some of the information you require may be protected under the seal of the confessional, so of course I cannot divulge it."

"Bishop Rush," she said, "withholding information in a murder inquiry — "

" — is not nearly so serious a matter as violating the trust between a penitent and his confessor."

"The penitent is dead," Harriet protested. "How can he possibly object?"

• The Perfection of his Failure •

"I did not say that the penitent in question was Father Sylvester."

Harriet was a quick study, and it did not take her long to arrive at a monstrous conclusion: "You know who killed him."

"I didn't say that."

"Let me tell you something, Bishop Rush." She stood and leaned across the desk. "If you think I'm going to allow you to sit there in your sacred silence with the name of a murderer on your lips, then you have seriously underestimated me and the system I serve." She leaned closer. "I can have you in an interrogation room in ten minutes, regardless of your relationship with the chief of police. I can detain you without warrant." She leaned closer still. "I can put you in a cell with men who won't think twice about violating your episcopal dignity. I can — "

"Actually, you can't, and we both know it." His confidence was infuriating. "Now, you'd better straighten up before you fall across my desk. Then you will allow me to answer the questions I can before vaulting to any more conclusions."

Harriet straightened up. "Good God," she asked the ceiling, "what is the world coming to when the prince of a corrupt and dying religion can hold the law to ransom?"

"Rumours of our death have been exaggerated," the bishop responded. "Would you like a cup of tea?"

"No, I wouldn't."

"Coffee?"

"No, thank you."

"Well, I would," and he rose and left the room.

Harriet took the opportunity to have a look around. She was surprised not to find a Bible on the desk, or in the shelves behind the desk. The latter were filled mostly with framed photographs of people Harriet did not recognize: married couples, newly ordained priests, men in black robes with feathered hats, women of various shapes and sizes, many of them wearing hats as well. There were people Harriet did recognize, too: civic leaders, the chief of police, the prime minister with his local member of Parliament.

The bishop returned some minutes later with a steaming mug with THE BOSS printed across it in block capitals. Harriet was startled, both by the mug and by its means of arrival. She had assumed that when a bishop wanted tea it was brought to him in a cup and saucer by some minor functionary, perhaps a nun. But he was speaking now as he sipped the scalding liquid.

"Ignatius Sylvester," the bishop was saying. "Yes, that was his real name. He was known as Iggy to his intimates. Well, poor Father Sylvester spent much of his adult life being shunted from one institution to another, one assignment to another. He was an embarrassment to the order. He had failed his doctorate shortly after ordination, and things went downhill from there. Long before he arrived in this diocese, he had become an addict of both nicotine and alcohol, and his idea of personal hygiene was eccentric, to put it mildly. It was here, however, that he finally met a local superior with the courage to tell him that his life was a shambles, and he stank. As I understand it, he was given the choice of going to a treatment centre or going to a treatment centre, if you take my meaning."

Harriet nodded.

"He went off crying intellectual rape," the bishop resumed, "but he returned six months later with new teeth — a marked improvement, I assure you — and to my knowledge he never took another drink. A year later he quit smoking, which stunned everyone who knew him. He never did catch on to the trick of washing regularly, but two out of three ain't bad, and considering his subsequent choice of vocation, it didn't really matter. As to his function in this diocese — "

"What do you mean," Harriet interrupted, "'his subsequent choice of vocation'?"

"I was coming to that." Bishop Rush would not be rushed. "I don't think Father Sylvester was ever a happy man. I suspect he wanted to be a farmer, like his father and brothers, but his mother had decided that one of her sons was going to be a priest, and Ignatius was it. He came from a generation whose mothers did that sort of thing, and sons went along with it. Alcohol and tobacco were merely his means of coping. They masked his despair. But once they were gone, there was nothing to prevent his demons from emerging, fully fanged and crying for vengeance."

"You have a colourful turn of phrase, Bishop Rush."

"It comes from exhorting sinners from the pulpit." He drained his cup. "Would you like a cup of tea now?"

"I wouldn't mind a coffee, actually," Harriet admitted.

"Good, I thought you were lying the last time."

She followed him out of the office.

"I'll get it," he said.

"I prefer to fix it myself."

"Are you afraid I'll poison you?"

He said it with such gravity that for an instant she wondered if he wasn't joking. The priesthood had always struck her as an extremely serious, if fundamentally irrational, business. She couldn't say such things out loud, but something deep within her rebelled at the thought of a priest having fun.

"Your Excellency!" cried a shrill voice, jolting the inspector from her thoughts. She turned to see a large-breasted woman of late middle age bearing down on them with a clipboard and a pen. His Excellency did not flinch, but maintained his course to the coffee stand.

"Father Andrew is waiting to hear if you'll concelebrate at his parents' fiftieth-anniversary mass."

"Let him wait," said Bishop Rush, plugging in an electric kettle.

"And the Priests' Senate meets in fifteen minutes."

"Let them start without me," he said. "They abuse me when I'm there, anyway."

The woman looked for a moment as if she might strangle him, then turned on her heel and marched away.

"That was Mrs. O'Halloran," said the bishop. "I inherited her from my predecessor."

"A formidable woman," Harriet remarked.

"No, Inspector. *You* are a formidable woman. *She* is a pest."

Harriet frowned. She wasn't sure she liked being thought of as formidable.

"I hope you don't mind," he said, rinsing out a ceramic teapot, "but I prefer tea, and it takes time to brew properly."

"Not at all," said Harriet.

"Help yourself." The bishop indicated a large thermos. "There is milk and cream in the fridge"— he indicated a compact structure beneath the table — "and honey and sugar on the counter."

Harriet chose a mug and poured coffee into it from the thermos. She waited as the bishop brewed his tea.

"Why did you insist on fixing it yourself," he inquired, "when you take it black?"

Harriet could have brazened it out, she supposed, and put cream and sugar in it, but she suspected His Excellency would see through that as easily as he was seeing through her ploy for having a wider look at the premises.

"I wanted to have a look around," she admitted. "Much of a police officer's job involves standing and waiting, but if you're not watching and listening while you're standing and waiting, your existence is a waste of time."

"A severely practical point of view," said the bishop, pouring his tea.

"You don't subscribe to it?"

"I do not. We are human be-ings, not human do-ings."

• The Perfection of his Failure •

"You were about to tell me," Harriet resumed, once they were back in the bishop's office, "about Father Sylvester's function in the diocese."

"So I was," said Bishop Rush, as if he were grateful to be reminded. "I don't know if you are familiar with the structure and governance of religious orders in the Catholic Church, but they are vast and varied, and each has its charism, or its gift. Some are teachers, some are health care workers, some preach, some work among the poor, some shut themselves off from the world to pray for the salvation of souls. Father Ignatius's order was founded, in the first instance, to educate young men for the priesthood. Over two centuries their charism has evolved to embrace adult education in general. The majority of Iggy's confrères are highly educated men who teach in colleges and universities. They have established, and in many cases still own, a number of institutions of higher education across North America."

Harriet noted that the bishop was referring to the dead priest more familiarly as his narrative progressed.

"This was not Iggy's cup of tea, and with his crutches kicked out from under him he could no longer pretend that it was. To the horror of his confrères, he found himself gravitating toward the people with whom he felt most comfortable: the poor, the weak, the luckless, the abandoned, the betrayed. The riches of the church, St. Laurence called them, and was roasted on a griddle for his impertinence. In short — "

"Roasted on a griddle?" Harriet could not let that go by. "What on earth are you talking about?"

"You don't know the legend of St. Laurence?" the bishop asked. Harriet didn't.

"The Emperor Valerian published edicts against the Christians in the third century. Within a year the pope was put to death, but on his way to execution he promised his deacon, Laurence, that he would follow him in three days. Laurence went to the prefect of the city and offered to show him the riches of the church. The prefect, believing that he was being offered a bribe, assented, and on the third day Laurence gathered all the lepers and beggars in the city and presented them to the prefect. These were, he said, the riches of the church, but the prefect was so outraged that he ordered Laurence to be placed on a gridiron, over glowing coals, to die a slow and painful death. The Romans were adept at executions — they invented crucifixion, after all — but Laurence cheerfully accepted his fate, and halfway through the ordeal asked his executioners to turn him over, for he was done on that side."

"Sounds a bit far-fetched," said Harriet.

"That's why we call it a legend."

"Are you comparing Father Sylvester to St. Laurence?"

"I am simply saying that he began keeping company with beggars and prostitutes. That might have been acceptable in a purely pastoral sense. It was when he began inviting them to the college for meals that his confrères rebelled.

"Don't misunderstand me, Inspector. These men own nothing personally. It would be unusual to find one with more than a few dollars in his pocket. As an order, however, they are rich as Croesus. They own land and buildings; they employ cooks and janitors and secretaries and housekeepers; they have credit cards and expense accounts and fully stocked larders, not to mention generous salaries as university professors."

He paused to take a sip of tea.

"A portion of each local house's income is taxed by the mother house, and a larger portion is distributed among various charities, but there is always more than enough left over. They are bachelors, after all. If you're earning a college president's salary, or a professor's, and you have no mortgage, no dependents, no personal expenses to speak of . . . well, you can see how a level of luxury might be attained almost without intention. Father Sylvester's mistake was in observing a certain inconsistency between lifestyle and vow, and opting for the latter."

"He decided to live in fact" — Harriet was beginning to catch on — "the poverty he had vowed in theory."

"That was when he came to me." The bishop nodded. "He wanted to know if I had some little thing for him to do in the west end that would keep him busy."

"Did you?"

"No, I didn't, and his local superior assured me that the worst thing I could do was set Iggy loose among the homeless and the abused. I suppose he thought the temptations would be too great for him. On the other hand, he could offer no alternative, except to keep him on a short leash until he could be transferred again and become someone else's responsibility. Can't blame him, really. People like Iggy were entirely beyond his experience."

The bishop shifted his weight in his chair.

"Now, you must understand, Inspector Linden, a bishop's role is primarily administrative, not pastoral, and Iggy was beyond my experience as well. Even so, I knew that his superior's solution was no solution at all. Iggy was done on that side, as St. Laurence might have put it. He was not a stupid man. He knew where temptation lay, and it wasn't among the walking wounded on Twentieth Street. No, if anything was going to drive him back to his addictions, it was the conscious charity of his confrères."

The bishop leaned back, tenting his fingers before him.

"From a practical point of view, the last thing any of us needed was a stinking drunk embarrassing himself and the church every time he opened his mouth, so it was as an administrator rather than a pastor, I fear, that I arranged to divert some funds to his cause and gave him permission to establish his ministry in the diocese."

"Which was . . . ?" Harriet prompted.

The bishop raised his hands, palms up. "The perfection of his failure."

"I don't understand."

"I'm not sure I do, either." Bishop Rush smiled apologetically. "All I know is, he rented a storefront in the inner city, bought a coffee urn and . . . other things . . . and he was in business."

"Other things?" Harriet prompted. It was the first time she had seen the bishop hesitate.

"Sanitary," the bishop said, carefully, "napkins."

"Excuse me," said Harriet, blushing in spite of herself. She had been raised in the belief that one did not advert to matters of feminine hygiene in mixed company. So had the bishop. "What on earth did he want with sanitary napkins?"

"You are not the first person to ask that question."

"I imagine not," said Harriet, and a silence fell between them. She finished her coffee and placed her mug on the bishop's desk. "You said he was in business. Surely he wasn't selling them."

"Of course not. I was speaking figuratively. But you asked about Father Sylvester's function in the diocese, and that was it. He handed out coffee and sanitary napkins. There is, apparently, a huge demand for both."

Harriet had to think about that. Coffee was the universal specific for drunkenness, loneliness, and despair, and the traditional adjunct to all manner of social intercourse. As to sanitary napkins, she could imagine few things more degrading than a poverty that would place them out of reach. She had never thought about it before.

"I trust," said the bishop, "that I have answered the who, what, and where of Iggy's ministry."

"Not quite," said Harriet. "Were you aware that he had been attacked before?"

• The Perfection of his Failure •

The bishop paused. "I was aware," he said, "that his lifestyle gave rise to certain dangers." He shifted in his chair. "I was aware that he was vulnerable."

"Were you aware that he had been stabbed at least twice before, and beaten?"

"I was not aware of specific circumstances."

"And you did nothing?"

"He asked me not to."

"*The perfection of his failure*, you said. What did you mean by that?"

"I can only guess, but from my perspective, the great success of Iggy's life was that he had failed at everything he tried. I don't mean to be cynical, or patronizing, but I think he was able to look back on his life and conclude that failing was the only thing he was really good at. Where better to prove it than among the cast-offs, the detritus of society? In the end, I suspect, he gravitated toward his own kind not because there was nowhere else to go but because it was, as I suggested, the perfection of his failure."

Smug bastard, thought Harriet.

"You disagree," said the bishop.

"He wasn't handing out sanitary napkins," she said. "He was handing out dignity."

⁘

The funeral was anything but the quiet affair Ignatius Sylvester's confrères had anticipated. Iggy had no family left, and few friends, but there was barely room in the chapel for the deceased, and the bishop had to admit that he might have made a mistake in insisting on a closed coffin, for many of the people he saw in the congregation looked worse in life than Ignatius Sylvester had in death. The halt and the lame, the haggard and the defeated, the walking wounded — the riches of the church — swelled the pews and overflowed into the aisles. The stench of unwashed bodies was as palpable as incense, it was almost intoxicating, and it was all Brendan Rush could do to remain present to the sacrament he was celebrating.

The bishop rarely presided at funerals. They depressed him, made him anxious. But he had made an exception in this case. The reasons were not entirely clear to him, but he knew they had something to do with his conversation with Inspector Linden — that and the brief confession he had heard one Saturday evening while taking his turn in one of the reconciliation rooms at the cathedral. He had refused absolution then, and he was prepared to refuse the sacrament now as he saw the man's troubled face in the congregation.

Inspector Linden, who invariably attended the funerals of the murdered, noticed the bishop's unease when the man went up to take communion, and watched the bishop refuse him. She wanted to make an arrest, but she knew the Crown would not support her. There was insufficient evidence, and the bishop would not break the seal of the confessional.

Trundling through the Glen

There was a familiar figure at the bank machine in South Kensington. I had seen him in Pimlico the day before, clothed in yellow from head to heel. Today he was wearing pink, from his suede laced boots to his bulging tights, a doublet surmounted by a tunic, and a feathered hat. He had attained nature's perfect proportion: a sphere.

He turned, stuffing £20 notes into a capacious wallet, also pink. Even his hair was pink: a thin fringe creeping out from under his hat, like slender fingers poised over a globe.

"Ah," he said, "you're the fellow on the bus."

I took a step backward. He took a step forward. When I had seen him the day before, he had been striding purposefully along Lower Sloane Street as I swept by in the top of a #11 bus. London being what it is, with its start-again, stop-again traffic, I swept by several times and each time watched him catch up and pass beneath my gaze as the vehicle ground to a halt in the congested roadway.

"You were wearing yellow then," I said.

"I think not," he said. "Mondays are blue, invariably."

"Mondays may be blue, but yesterday was Tuesday and you were wearing yellow."

"You didn't see me on Monday?"

A pair of buses dieseled past, temporarily drowning conversation. I thought back to the day in question. I had been in Roper's Garden in Chelsea most of the afternoon, shooting a wedding party. It took longer than I had anticipated, for a pair of homeless men kept showing up in the background, and the bride's father eventually had to pay them off to make them go away. Afterward, I walked up Old Church Street to the King's Road, where I took a bus to the Sloane Square Tube station. I was late for an appointment, and anxious, for I dislike going underground, but I'm sure I would have noticed a spherical blue man along the way.

"I am used to being noticed," he said. "Most people aren't, and when it is pointed out to them, they resent it."

"What do they resent," I asked, "not being noticed or being told they're not used to it?"

"What they resent," he said, with a conspiratorial incline of his head, "is being noticed in their turn by someone who looks like me."

There was a great deal of truth in what he said, but I was anxious to use the bank machine. I had to circumnavigate his equator to do so, for he was disinclined to move.

"As you have no doubt divined," he said, closing his shoulder bag with a dexterous twist of the clasp, "the bulk of my income is reserved for my wardrobe."

I had divined no such thing, but it came as no surprise. A body of that span would be expensive to clothe — doubly expensive in the *outré* manner he had chosen as his personal style. What did come as a surprise was that he should have noticed me, as I had noticed him, and that on two consecutive days one of us had noticed the other without the other knowing it.

"You are not a Londoner," he said.

"I've lived here for seventeen years," I said over my shoulder.

"But your accent is not native to these shores, I believe."

I retrieved my card and cash, and turned to find that he still had not moved. "I'm from Canada," I told him.

"Ah, well," he said. "No need to apologize."

"I wasn't going to."

"Well, perhaps you should." He narrowed his eyes and cocked one eyebrow, suggesting that he had not only looked into my mind but disapproved of something he found there. "If you are not from London, nor am I to be found in Sherwood Forest, robbing the rich to give to the poor."

A Porsche and a Bentley swept past. The Porsche had been tuned for performance rather than silence, but the Bentley whispered by with barely a shiver in the air.

"So what's with the neo-mediæval-disco-revival clothing?" I asked.

"You have a colourful turn of phrase," he said. "I am, in fact, wearing what are called split hose. They are made of a specially woven twill which is extremely elastic. Each leg, as you can see" — he stepped back to show me — "has a seam running up the back. They are lined with linen to mid-thigh, with eyelets on the upper edge to attach to the doublet."

He lifted his tunic in illustration, and I was pleased to see a large codpiece guarding his modesty. I wasn't pleased to see the codpiece, particularly, but the alternative would have been unpleasant. Two women driving past in a Mini honked enthusiastically.

"Don't imagine I don't know what you're thinking," he said. "*He may dress like Robin Hood, but he is constructed along the lines of Friar Tuck.*"

The thought had crossed my mind.

"You will scarcely be amazed, then," he continued, "when I tell you that my name is Tuck. Vernon John Tuck." He extended a plump hand. It would have been churlish to refuse it, but I dreaded what would follow. Having told me his name, he expected me to return the courtesy.

"Hood," I said, clearing my throat.

"Hood?"

"Uhm . . . Robin, as a matter of fact . . . Robin Hood."

"You jest, sir." He fixed me with a stern eye. "You mock me."

"My friends call me Rob," I said, and handed him a business card.

"I'm sure they do" — he glanced at the card with brief contempt — "but I do not count myself among them," and he turned on his heel and strode away.

"What are the chances, do you think," I asked my friend Tristan later that evening, "of seeing the same person two days in a row?"

"Pretty good, I should think." Tristan had a degree in philosophy and drove a taxi for a living; what he had not seen on the streets of London he had likely imagined. "I frequently see you three or four days in a row."

"Yes, but we live in the same building, we go to the same shops. What if it's a total stranger and you see him one day in Pimlico, say, and the next day in South Kensington?"

"I'm sure it happens all the time," said Tristan, "but most people don't notice. I once saw a bald-headed girl with a green topknot in Charing Cross, and later the same day I saw her thirty miles away outside the gender clinic in Bishop's Stortford. The only reason I noticed was because of her topknot. I doubt that she noticed me."

"But this man noticed me, too, and it was on a day that I didn't notice him."

"So it's happened three days in a row?"

I nodded. "He saw me on a bus on Monday in Chelsea, I saw him from a bus on Tuesday in Pimlico, and today I met him at a bank machine in South Kensington."

"Are you sure it's the same man?"

"Oh, yes," I said, and described him. "His name is Tuck."

"Now you're being deliberately provocative," said Tristan.

"Vernon John Tuck," I assured him. "I gave him my business card."

"How did he react?"

"Not well."

"Serves you right," said Tristan. "I've told you to change your name."

"There's nothing wrong with my name."

It was a name to trade on, in fact. Many people who called my studio out of vulgar curiosity or the urge to mock eventually retained my professional services for the weddings, anniversaries, birthdays, and family portraits that are my bread and butter. "Robin Hood took the pictures," they will say.

"The real Friar Tuck was named Alfred," said Tristan.

"There was no real Friar Tuck," I said. "It was a TV show."

"Your round, I believe."

"Do you mind?" I asked, patting my pockets. "I seem to have left my wallet at home."

"Now, there's a surprise."

Home was a flat in Maida Vale, where I had given over the largest of my three bedrooms to the computers, scanners, printers, and software attendant on digital technology. The smallest of the bedrooms, little more than a closet, was light-safe, and it was there I did the darkroom work for the few projects that still required film. I sometimes set up lights and a backdrop in the living room, converting it temporarily to an old-fashioned photographer's studio, but mostly I worked on site, in natural light. I did my books on a laptop computer on an antique roll-top desk in the living room. It was there, five days later, that I received the call.

"Hood," he said.

"Tuck," I responded, for I recognized his voice.

"We must meet."

"Why?"

"Do you know the Bridge House in Little Venice?"

"Of course," I said. "It's fifteen minutes from my flat."

"Tomorrow," he said, "seven o'clock," and rang off.

"What should I do?" I asked Tristan when I met him later on the stairs.

"You can't not go," he said. "Natural curiosity alone would compel one to attend the rendezvous. It would me." A conspiratorial look came into his eye. "Do you want backup?"

"What for?"

"With people like that, you never know when things might turn ugly, and no one notices a taxi in the street."

"Everyone notices a taxi in the street. Most people try to get into it."

"I could take photographs," he suggested.

I reminded him that I was the photographer. Still, I wasn't entirely comfortable with the situation, and I accepted his offer.

"Don't forget your wallet," he said.

"I still can't find it," I told him.

I assumed that Tuck would be dressed in yellow, and I was not disappointed. As I crossed the footbridge over the canal at Westbourne Terrace Road, I saw him in the forecourt, a bright sunspot against the pale pink of the inn. He raised a hand in greeting, but he did not smile. He was holding a liqueur glass with a startling yellow liquid in it. I went inside and ordered a pint of IPA before joining him. I was aware of the curious eyes of the other drinkers on us as we seated ourselves at one of the outdoor tables. There was a modest crowd for a Tuesday evening, but we had the table to ourselves.

"They stare," said Tuck, "but they do not understand."

"Neither do I."

"I've looked you up. It seems you are authentic."

"I'm relieved to hear it."

"Synchronicity."

"I beg your pardon?"

"Christians call it providence, atheists call it coincidence, Jungians call it synchronicity. But I think it is no coincidence that, in a city of ten million souls, you and I should have been thrown together like thistles in a wheat field."

"I don't quite follow," I said.

"I imagined I was appealing to your agrarian sympathies," he said: "Canada, wheat, thistles. Perhaps I was mistaken."

"I still don't follow."

"Do you deny that you were in Abbey Road yesterday morning?"

I saw no reason to deny it. It had been a profitable few hours. The famous zebra crossing by the EMI studio where the Beatles recorded *Abbey Road* remains popular among clients of all ages. On Monday morning a family of four — mother, father, and two adult daughters dressed in character as John, Paul, George, and Ringo — had determinedly crossed and re-crossed the road while I endeavoured to capture a digital facsimile of the album cover. They ordered a hundred glossy colour prints, at £5 each, for friends and family back in Japan.

"I didn't see you," I said.

"I was loath to reveal myself."

"I don't think I've ever met anyone who was less loath to reveal himself," I said.

"Mock me if you will," he said, raising his glass and one eyebrow in tandem, "but I could not take the chance that you might think I was following you."

In an instant, his plan became clear. The series of unlikely coincidences that had brought this twelfth-century pantomime monk into my life had nothing to do with synchronicity or providence. This Tuck person — and I had only his word for it that his name *was* Tuck — had obviously seen one of my advertisements and sought me out — to what purpose, I did not know, but I was grateful that Tristan was lurking around the corner.

Tuck took a thoughtful sip of his drink, and a moue of distaste visited his lips. "Limoncello," he said. "One can't get used to it, somehow, but it is the only beverage that matches the day's hue."

"You've been following me," I accused.

"*J'accuse?*" he said, and laughed quietly. "My dear Hood, unlike me, you are a rather ordinary-looking chap. You are half a head taller than I, which makes you about average in height. You have brown hair and brown eyes, and, to judge by your gently expanding girth, you are a little out of shape, although you fondly imagine that walking four or five miles a week will return you to the slim physiognomy of your youth. It won't, I assure you. The point is, you are virtually indistinguishable from a thousand other men who live within walking distance of this public house. Why on earth would a man like me want to follow a man like you?"

"Because my name is Robin Hood."

He waved a hand dismissively. "You might as well tell your friend to come out in the open," he said, as Tristan's taxi edged forward from Warwick Crescent. "He's not fooling anybody."

Tristan's designs would have been thwarted, in any case, as half a dozen revelers erupted from the Bridge House and piled into the back of his taxi, urging him to seek an address in St. John's Wood. He gave me an apologetic wave as he engaged his meter and drove away. A fare was a fare, after all. It was his livelihood.

"You need fear no unpleasantness from me," Tuck spoke into my thoughts. "By the same token, you needn't deny you were at Chelsea Town Hall Thursday afternoon."

That had been another wedding, with a jolly little rich father and a score of beautiful friends gathered to celebrate. After the ceremony, I joined the bridal party in a chartered boat on the Thames. The bride and her husband posed on the afterdeck as I took photographs, Tower Bridge looming in the background. Another profitable few hours in London. But I had seen nothing of Tuck, either at the hall or on the boat.

"A handsome couple," said Tuck, "and a beautiful day for a wedding." A cunning look came into his eyes. "I've sent them a present." He paused for effect. "A bottle of Chartreuse."

It was a challenge, which I met on the same breath: "You wear green on Thursdays."

"Very good, Robin Hood." He seemed pleased by his little rhyme. "What do you imagine I drink on Fridays?"

"Why do you imagine I care?"

"It's my favourite day of the week," said Tuck.

"Bloody Marys," I threw out.

He looked impressed, and took another sip of his Limoncello.

For what it was worth, I now had his weekday colour scheme: Mondays were blue, Tuesdays yellow, Wednesdays pink, Thursdays green, and Fridays red. I hadn't seen Tuck on Friday, and I was certain that he hadn't seen me. I had spent the hours of daylight in my flat, PhotoShopping scenes from the two weddings I'd shot that week and wondering where I had misplaced my wallet. It wasn't a major inconvenience because I was familiar with my failings and always carried cash in my camera bag. Still, it was vexing, and when I made a precautionary call to my bank they insisted on cancelling my cards and issuing new ones, which I hadn't bothered to pick up yet. I knew full well that, as soon as I did, my wallet would turn up — in the laundry, perhaps, or in a different camera bag. I had once found it behind a carton of eggs in the refrigerator.

On Friday evening, Tristan and I had gone to a fringe play in the back room of a pub in Islington, where the pair of us made up half the audience, if you included the author and her agent. The most memorable part of the evening was the harrowing ride home on the Tube from Angel Station. I am a confirmed surface dweller, and the deeper I go underground the more uneasy I become.

"Angel Station is a torment to the nerves," Tuck agreed, again speaking into my thoughts. "You step onto the longest escalators in Western Europe, which take you deep into the bowels of the earth and deliver you to the very suburbs of Dante's *Inferno*."

"Hampstead is deeper," I said.

"Holly Bush Hill is even deeper."

"What do you wear on weekends?"

"*At the weekend*," he said, correcting my Canadian usage, "I rarely get out of bed."

"Why?"

"I am a man of limited means, Robin Hood. The truth is, I can't afford to go out at the weekend."

"You could dress like Friar Tuck," I said. "A simple cassock, a pair of sandals . . ."

"Yes, but that would be boring."

I had a sudden insight. "Like . . . not being Robin Hood?"

"Exactly," said Tuck, with a nod. "I see that fate has dealt us each the same cruel hand."

I drained my pint and went inside for another. A table of wits by the window was lustily singing the Robin Hood song. There were just at the "feared by the bad, loved by the good" bit when one of the barmen told them to pipe down, this wasn't Monty-bloody-Python's Flying Circus.

"I see we have caused a stir," said Tuck as I rejoined him on the terrace.

"*You* have caused a stir," I corrected him. "I'm just an ordinary-looking chap, indistinguishable from a thousand other men who live within walking distance of this pub."

"You shouldn't undervalue yourself," he said, downing the last of his Limoncello.

"What do you do," I asked, "that keeps you in peculiar comfort five days a week but confines you indoors *at the weekend?*"

He hesitated, wondering if he should entrust me with the information.

"Normally, I do not answer that question," he said, "but there is obviously more to this than meets the eye." He paused again, and made a minute adjustment to his tunic. "I am, in a very modest way, a thief."

The look on my face made him laugh out loud — a deep, hearty laugh that shook his belly and chins. I wished I could have photographed it, for I think it was the first time he had been truly honest with me. He reached into his bag and handed out my wallet.

"Where did you get this?" I demanded.

"It was in your pocket."

"No, it wasn't. I haven't been able to find it since — " The truth struck me like a blow to the solar plexus. "You stole it at the bank machine!"

"You practically handed it to me," said Tuck, "and now I have handed it back."

I checked the contents. It was all there: cards, cash, ID. "I don't understand," I said.

"Neither do I," Tuck admitted. "Normally, I would have pocketed the cash and dropped the wallet in a letter box, trusting that the post office would eventually get it back to you. I don't deal in plastic. It's too risky, and I am not a greedy man. But you told me your name and gave me your card, and I already had your wallet. I couldn't give it back without serious embarrassment and possible legal consequences, so I walked away. But you kept turning up. Wherever I went, there you were. As I've said, there is more to this than meets the eye."

What met my eye, at that moment, was a disturbance at the table by the window inside the pub. One of the men had risen and was gesticulating with both hands. Voices were raised. The words were unintelligible, but their tenor was clearly one of outrage.

"What's going on in there?" I wondered.

"I imagine," said Tuck, "that it's his round, and he's discovered that his wallet is missing."

"You didn't . . ." I said.

"I did," said Tuck, patting his bag. "They chose to mock me when I arrived, so I had a little chat with them at their table."

"And you robbed them?"

"Only one of them. I am not a greedy man."

Four pairs of suspicious eyes stared out the window.

"Perhaps it's time we left," said Tuck.

"We?" I said. "You're the one they'll come after once they've put two and two together and come up with the fat man on the terrace."

"Personal remarks are not in good taste."

"I'm as much a victim as they are."

"A nice point," said Tuck, "but one, I fear, that they will be incapable of appreciating. They have already put two and two together and come up with you and me."

I watched as the four men pushed their chairs back and made for the door.

"Come," said Tuck with a gesture. People made way for us as we left, but they soon closed in behind. Tuck had to turn sideways to squeeze through the gate that led down to the canal, but we were already moving along the towpath when the men emerged from the pub, baying like hounds.

"We can't hope to outrun them," I said, though I was having difficulty keeping up with Tuck's determined strides.

• Trundling Through the Glen •

"There is no need to outrun them. All we have to do is outwit them."

We could not long sustain our flight without attracting attention, and we soon had an appreciative audience marking our progress. A narrow boat chugged by, spewing diesel exhaust along the towpath. Three lads fishing looked up with a wild surmise as we passed. Tuck closed in on the water and made as if to jump between two moored boats. Two of the fisher lads leapt up to stop him, but Tuck did not need to be stopped. He tossed his feathered cap into the canal, where it floated amid the styrofoam scraps and the plastic wrappers, the yellow hair spreading out like the tentacles of a jellyfish. He was entirely bald.

Looking back as we moved off the towpath, I saw that a small crowd had gathered at the canal's edge, staring at Tuck's floating hat as if they expected his bobbing head to appear amid the plumes of exhaust and the detritus of a consumer society.

"Bless this house and all who dwell within!" Tuck bellowed as he opened the door of a council flat and walked in. We had doubled back, confusing another portion of the crowd. From what I could see from the doorway, our pursuers had dwindled to the original four, who were the only ones who had any real interest in the affair, anyway. I followed Tuck inside, where a man in his underwear looked up from his television program, a cigarette dangling from his lips.

"My name is Robin Hood," I told him, for no particular reason.

A slim black woman appeared from the kitchen and pointed to the back door, whereby, she advised in a thick Welsh accent, we would get the fuck out if we knew what was good for us. Tuck nodded his thanks and we left.

We found ourselves in a communal wasteland, a drier version of the canal, with a disemboweled motorcycle leaning on a kickstand over its scattered organs. The sounds of pursuit grew louder.

"Where are they, the thieving cunts?"

"The fat one's mine!"

"They want your blood," I remarked.

"They would be just as satisfied with yours," said Tuck.

"Let us in!" someone bellowed at the front door.

"I'm an innocent bystander," I said.

Tuck opened the back door. "I invite you to debate the point with our hostess."

"Are you out of your mind?"

I slammed the door shut, but it was too late.

"There they are, the bastards!"

"Out of the way, mother!"

Two of them broke past the woman of the house, only to be met by the man of the house, who by this time was properly enraged. He may have dismissed Tuck and me as hallucinations, but these four appeared to be made of flesh and breakable bone, a theory he proceeded to test. It bought us some time.

"Take off your shirt," said Tuck, bending down to scoop up a handful of black oil from the motorcycle crankcase.

I heard a scream inside the flat. I took off my shirt. Tuck smeared my torso with the oil and told me to squat. I squatted. When two of the men broke through to the back door — one of them clutching his ear, which was bleeding heavily — I stood, calmly, and said, "What the fuck d'you want?"

"Where's the fat bastard?"

"The yellow-breasted shite!"

I had never seen a living thing as angry as these two men. I wondered that their flesh could contain it. I looked round the yard, coolly massaging a spot of oil into my navel. "Don't see anyone what matches that description."

"Out here!" someone yelled inside the flat. "The bastards went the other way!"

The two men went back inside the flat. I heard flesh smacking flesh and furniture turning over. There were shouts of anger and shrieks of pain, but the situation seemed to resolve itself into a tactical retreat as I heard the front door slam and the unmistakable howl of someone who has been struck on the back of the head with a chair.

Tuck opened his shoulder bag and took out a package of Handi-Wipes. "Clean yourself up," he said. "You look disgusting."

"Where did you go?"

"I didn't go anywhere. They chose not to see me, is all."

"You can't expect me," I said, wiping at the oil on my torso, "to believe that."

Tuck handed me another scented napkin. The viscous liquid smeared and thinned, but it would take a hot shower with strong soap to get the stuff off.

"You can believe what you like," said Tuck. "The fact remains that a half-naked man with oil on his belly is far more believable to the British male than someone who looks like me. I suspect they were positively relieved to find you alone back here."

"They didn't look it," I said. "I was afraid for my life."

"Then you should go on the stage," said Tuck, "for I have never seen anyone give a more convincing performance of *not* being afraid for his life."

"Yes, well, it was totally out of character," I said, and I found myself shaking in reaction. "And you were watching from where, exactly?"

Before Tuck could answer, the couple whose home we had invaded stepped out the back door, the yearning for justice palpable in their eyes. The woman was holding a butcher knife in one hand and rolling what may have been an earlobe between the thumb and fingers of the other. The man stood in his Y-fronts, brandishing a chair leg.

"My good woman," said Tuck, "I fear we have disrupted your evening. Here" — he took a wallet from his shoulder bag and began counting out banknotes — "I trust this will cover the damages. And you, my good man," he said, handing over the wallet itself, "should find enough plastic in there to keep you entertained until the gentlemen whose scalp you recently opened with that chair leg thinks to call his bank. With any luck, you will have withdrawn the maximum allowable out of each of his accounts by then. The number 2365 will give you access."

The woman was counting the cash, leaving a smear of blood on each note. "There's over two hundred quid here," she said.

"What the fu — " the man began, but Tuck silenced him with a raised forefinger. "All you have to remember is 2365."

"2365," said the man, "2365."

"Write it down, Alf," said the woman. "Try not to act as stupid as you look."

Alf took no offence, but instead looked up in a kind of wonder. "Thanks, guv," he said.

"Don't thank me," said Tuck. "Thank Robin Hood here."

"Robbin' from the rich to give to the poor," said Alf, with obvious approval, and the pair of them retired to their flat.

"How did you know the guy's PIN?" I asked later, as we retreated by quiet streets.

"I made it up," said Tuck.

"Alf isn't going to be happy when he finds out you lied to him."

"Probably not," Tuck agreed, "but I doubt that anyone offered him happiness in the first place. He'll put it down to his own stupidity, and so will that Welsh harridan he lives with. They're more than £200 to the good, in any case, which isn't a bad haul for an evening's work. Speaking of which," he said, handing me my wallet, "you'll be wanting this back."

I patted my pockets. "You stole it *again?*"

"It's really quite easy, once you know how. And if you don't mind my saying so, you are a very easy mark."

I minded very much, but there was no point in challenging him, the statement was so obviously true.

"Have you never been robbed before?"

"Not to my knowledge," I said, opening my wallet. It was empty. "What have you done with my money?"

"You don't seriously believe a man like that carries £200 in his wallet on a week night, do you?"

"So you felt free to hand out mine."

"It seemed better than being disemboweled with a butcher knife," said Tuck.

We walked in silence for a time.

"Are you magic?" I asked.

He smiled, then stroked his dome wistfully. "I'll miss that hat."

The Sins of the Fathers

"The point of object lessons," said Alison, "is that they have a point — an object — presumably for the practical or moral edification of the child. If parents simply pass them on from one generation to the next because their own parents did it, then object lessons take on the character of purposeless punishment."

Alison believes that I grew up in spite of my parents. She says that I observed them and listened to them, and unconsciously decided not to emulate them. I was a subversive child, and I agree that I probably learned more by contradiction than instruction, but I would judge my parents less harshly. I have learned, in any case, that it is pointless as an adult to try to redress the grievances of childhood.

When I first took Alison home to meet my family, she had the temerity to disagree with my father on a point of opinion. He was taken aback, but rose to the occasion with vigour. It is nonsense, of course, to offer firm opinions on things about which one knows little, if anything, but to men of my father's generation it was more acceptable to defend an untenable position than to admit ignorance on the matter in the first place.

My mother, on the other hand, was given to grieving over the injustices of her own childhood and happily re-inflicting them on her children. I remember telling Alison how, as a five-year-old, I came home one day with a bouquet of flowers and proudly presented them to my mother. My father always gave her flowers on her birthday, and her pleasure on those occasions was palpable.

"Oh dear," she said, raising one eyebrow, "where did you get these?"

"I found them."

"Where?"

"In the alley."

"Were they growing in a row?"

I suspected this was a trick question, but I lacked the subtlety of thought to see what difference it made, so I told her the truth.

"Alvie," she said, "that's *stealing*."

I knew enough about stealing that the only thing likely to get me out of it was a stout denial. I knew enough about lying to regret it immediately. I knew nothing at all about object lessons.

I knocked on the back door of the little one-storey house across the alley, my left hand clutching the purloined flowers, my right hand compressed in a tear-stained fist. I could not be sure that my mother had telephoned the old lady who lived there — "Alvie's on his way over, Mrs. Kuzik; you may beat him if you like" — but I wasn't prepared to take the chance that she hadn't.

As the door opened, I held out the flowers and closed my eyes. "I'm sorry but I picked these and gave them to my mum and I didn't know they were yours I'm sorry I won't do it again."

I was expecting Mrs. Kuzik to be at least as upset as my mother. They were her flowers, after all, planted and watered and carefully tended through the dry heat of summer. Instead, she folded her warm, ancient hands around my fist and said, "Take them home to your mother and tell her to put them in water."

I dropped them in the alley. I have not since given flowers to any woman, not even Alison. The fact that my grandmother had once done the same thing to my mother did not strike my mother as ironic, although she related the story with bitter amusement at a family gathering years afterward.

"I thought it was you that happened to," said Alison later.

I suppose my parents suffered at the hands of their own parents, for the adult conspiracy against children is as old as the Bible. Abraham appeared willing to sacrifice his only son, Isaac, to demonstrate his obedience to God, and God himself sent his only son to the cross to redeem miserable humankind. As a parent myself, I cannot help but think that humankind would not be nearly so miserable if only we treated our children better. If a disembodied voice had told me to take my child up a mountain and slit her throat, I would have told that voice to take a flying fuck at a frisbee. I would sooner slit my own throat. One can only imagine Isaac's subsequent attitude toward his aging parent: ambivalent, at best.

My parents both sprang from a line of Scottish teetotallers, and the Scots do nothing by halves. My maternal grandmother, in her late 70s, was advised of a folk remedy for arthritis that involved soaking a clove of garlic in a pint of gin and taking a nip before bed each evening. In the recommended dosage, I reckoned it would take her four months to polish off the bottle. But she was mortally afraid of acquiring a taste for the stuff, and decided not to step onto that slippery slope. She died in her 80s, in pain, and without ever knowing the taste of alcohol.

My paternal grandmother, similarly, based her faith on the dubious virtue of sobriety. Among her effects after she died, my father and his brothers found a bottle of something called Hospital Gin. "For Medicinal Use," it advised on the label, but throughout her life neither marriage, war, childbirth, nor death had produced an occasion grave enough to open the bottle. When my grandfather's physician prescribed stout for his ailing heart, judging that a pint or two of Guinness a day would materially alter his outlook on life, my grandmother dutifully arranged for a slightly seedy individual of her acquaintance to procure a bottle. She kept it in the fridge and allowed my grandfather two teaspoons a day. She lived a widow, alone and lonely, for twenty years afterward.

Unimpressed by this matrilineal spirit of temperance, my parents nevertheless decided that liquor, although not evil in itself, should be concealed from their children. They drank prodigiously, but only after dark and behind closed doors. My mother developed a tone of voice that precluded contradiction. When she said, "Your father and I are going to bed," we took it to mean that she loved us dearly, but she loved our father more, and anyone who disturbed them would be shot. As the four of us children, in turn, achieved puberty and grim knowledge, we thought we finally understood what was going on up there. We didn't, but as I grew up and settled into a comfortable position as the host of an afternoon radio program, I arrived at a certain philosophical attitude regarding my own children. So when Fred Fairley came to my door one Saturday afternoon and accused my daughter Annie of picking the blossoms off his hybrid roses and eating them, I told him to take a flying fuck at a frisbee.

"She was *seen!*" Fred protested.

"By whom?"

I had no doubt of Annie's guilt, for I had smelt the fragrant crime on her breath, but I was not about to give Freddy the satisfaction of his righteousness. It turned out, as I had expected, that his information came second-hand from local busybodies: Old Horrocks across the alley, a semi-retired mortician, and the widow Grazely three doors down. No doubt he was vexed to be morally disarmed by someone in the media, but his indignation was compounded by the realization that, far from joining the adult conspiracy, I was prepared to defend my daughter against it.

I knew Freddy of old. We grew up in the same neighbourhood. We attended the same crumbling brick schools. Freddy was a lean boy with a narrow face and a nose as sharp as a fox. It took little imagination to see him in the mind's eye making for a quiet place in the woods with some limp, helpless creature dangling from his jaws. "I dined on rodent this afternoon," he would say. "Grain fed. The flesh was tender and sweet."

It was malignant fate that had made us neighbours again as adults, for the Fairley clan were a toxic breed, and neither Frederick nor his brother, Vernon, had learned much from the sins of their own father. They were raised in a household where stupid questions were labelled as such and the questioner appropriately ridiculed. They often appeared at school with bruises. Their mother we rarely saw.

From this early training, Freddy and Vern had each aspired to positions of authority. Vernon was a communications officer with the police service, and he made no secret of the fact that he intended to wear an inspector's uniform one day. "Better start checking the costume shops, then," his father advised, before expiring from a brief but brutally painful heart attack. Freddy went in for the priesthood, and for a while he strutted about in a Roman collar, but he was laicized soon after burying his father. I suspect he realized it was never going to get any better than that. Now he sold insurance. While their contemporaries were busy mating and breeding, Freddy and Vern remained single and childless, but that didn't stop them from trying to punish other people's children.

"You haven't heard the last of this," Freddy warned as I closed the door in his face.

"You're so sexy when you're abusing the neighbours," Alison remarked as she came in from the back yard. "What was that about?"

"He says Annie's been eating his roses."

"I was wondering why she smelt like that."

When I confronted Annie, a darkly beautiful child, then four years old, she readily admitted her guilt.

"Why did you do it?" I asked.

"They looked so *good*," she replied, and burst into tears.

"And were they?"

"No!" she sobbed. "They tasted awful!"

"But you kept on eating them," I said, "because you thought the next one might taste better?"

She nodded.

"Well, you'd better stop now," I said. "They're probably laced with pesticide."

She nodded again, and looked up through her tears, much as I must have looked up at Mrs. Kuzik those many years ago. "Am I going to die, Daddy?"

"Not before me, sweetheart," I assured her. "It's against the rules," and there the matter might have rested had it not been for Fred Fairley's outraged sense of justice.

The first thing I noticed was the police cars. Normally, we might see two or three a month along our quiet crescent, but now they passed the house daily, sometimes hourly, an alert officer behind the wheel. I remembered how the police used to cruise our old neighbourhood, periodically banishing us from the grassy median that separated the north- and south-bound lanes of the street. For reasons that were never explained to us, children were forbidden to play there. The police officers urged us to go to the nearby public playground. When we explained that the playground in question was littered with broken glass and cigarette butts, and that anyone younger and weaker than the thugs who had claimed it as their turf was likely to be beaten, the officers were unmoved. And so, heaving great sighs and rolling our eyes, we would vacate the space, wait two or three minutes, and then resume our play. It was rare to be caught twice on the same day, for the police usually had better things to do in that quarter of the city. An unusually bored constable once waited ten minutes before returning, and the six of us who had been playing football on the boulevard scattered like flushed rabbits. That was the first time I heard the expression, "Take a flying fuck at a frisbee!" Vern Fairley tossed it over his shoulder at the pursuing officer as we made our escape into the warren of lanes and gardens behind the houses of our inner-city neighbourhood.

We used to call them the Fairley Stupid Brothers. Freddy was always a bit of a dickhead, but I had expected better things from Vern — Sergeant Vernon Fairley, as he now was — for it was obvious that Freddy's big brother was behind the sudden, oppressive police presence on our crescent. If I had observed and rejected the sins of my parents, Freddy and Vern had absorbed theirs and vowed vengeance on the rest of the world.

One Monday morning as Alison left for work she found a ticket on her windshield — for parking in the same location for longer than twenty-four hours, in contravention of an obscure bylaw passed by a horse-drawn civic administration in the previous century. It was Alison's habit, after a week of teaching and committee work, to park her Neon on Friday afternoon and leave it there until she needed it again Monday morning. By becoming a one-car family two days a week, we hoped to make some small contribution toward conserving the earth's resources. When I called Parking Enforcement, the officer cited the bylaw and assured me that it allowed for no exceptions.

Two can play at this game, I thought, and responded with a commentary on my radio program. "This bylaw," I said, "is both old and stupid. Those who passed it were already a generation behind the times. Those who enforce it are misguided. Surely the police have better things to do than monitor the parking habits of productive citizens when sexual slavery is rampant in the west end."

I watched my producer gesticulating at the console as I spoke, but this was live radio and there was nothing he could do about it. Even so, the talk-back lines were jammed for hours, and neither of us was prepared for the avalanche of email that followed. A few were from inner-city workers who lauded my attempt to draw attention to the issue of sexual exploitation among children and teenage girls, but the majority were from irate citizens. Oddly, most of them were more concerned about parking.

"I suppose you think you can park wherever you please," read one. "Thank God the police are there to keep malcontents like you in line."

"I'll bet you're the one who's always taking my spot," read another. "I'm calling the cops next time for sure."

"You're probably upset because you don't have a parking space of your own," read another, "and just because you're not getting any," the writer went on, finally touching on the sex issue, "doesn't mean that you can impugn the reputation of this beautiful city!"

"He's wrong on several points," I informed my producer, Ernie. "First, I *do* have my own parking space. Second, I'm getting plenty. Third — "

Ernie held up a hand. "I don't want to hear about it."

The story passed to the newsroom. Everyone knew there were sometimes underage kids turning tricks on 20th Street, but that hardly warranted the sweeping indictment I had made.

"Why haven't we heard about this before?" one reporter asked.

"Because the corporate culture that controls the mainstream media doesn't want you to know about it," I said.

"What are your sources?" demanded another, and I handed him a copy of a weekly newspaper I had picked up at the back of the cathedral on Sunday. On page one there was a story about global human trafficking. On page three there was a story about a Ukrainian organization whose sole purpose was rescuing children from the sex trade. On page eight a nun from the diocesan social justice office explained how small Canadian cities were ideal portals for the transportation of human beings in the international slave trade. "Trafficking in children," she was quoted as saying, "is as lucrative as smuggling drugs. Over a million human beings are sold into sexual slavery every year, and half of them are children."

The news director decided to run the story in the next slot, and other media outlets soon picked it up. Sergeant Vernon Fairley responded at a media briefing the following day. He tried to downplay the story. "Perhaps Mr. MacKay forgot to take his medication that morning," he quipped.

"Of course you know," I said to Alison, "this means war."

"Can't you let it go, Alvie? You've made your point."

"I'll let it go," I said, "if you'll stop arguing with my father."

She said she would support me in whatever I decided to do.

People normally tuned in to my program for local news and weather, music, concert and theatre reviews, interviews, and eclectic commentaries from their host. Now a whole new demographic was showing up in the ratings. Over the next few weeks the station ran a series of stories on teen prostitution, bolstered by interviews with inner-city social workers and a five-minute documentary about a gang of priests on 20th Street who offered food and sanctuary to the homeless and the abused. When I interviewed a thirteen-year-old prostitute who claimed she was worth $5,000 a week to the pimp that owned her, I was invited to the police station to reveal my sources. Vernon Fairley glanced up from his desk as I walked by.

"You didn't cuff him?" he asked the escorting officer.

"He isn't charged with anything."

"Yet," said Fairley.

Even a tame journalist like me has the right to protect his sources, and I didn't want to put the girl's life at risk, so I told them nothing. They were vexed, but in the end they had to admit that I had committed no crime. They insinuated that child prostitution had not been nearly such a problem before I started sticking my nose in where it didn't belong. I responded with another commentary.

Outraged citizens remained outraged, but our broadcasts did have the effect of redirecting a portion of their abuse to the authorities who had allowed the situation to develop. Questions were asked in city council and the provincial legislature, but mayor and premier alike were hopelessly uninformed. The chief of police declared that his department was monitoring the situation, but could not explain to anyone's satisfaction exactly what that meant. Meanwhile, a group of concerned citizens took clipboards onto "the stroll" where, to the vast annoyance of the working girls, they recorded the license numbers of passing cars, which they proposed to publish in an attempt to shame the business out of existence.

The sex trade flourished, of course, and business picked up for the priests who ministered in the inner city. An appeal went out for donations. Most media outlets ran it as a public service. Eventually, a visibly peeved Vernon Fairley announced at his weekly press briefing that a task force had been struck to look into the situation.

"We can't have vigilantes taking matters into their own hands," he said, "on the advice of some glorified disk jockey."

The patrol cars kept cruising by our house, and Alison moved her Neon every twenty-four hours to avoid another ticket. Annie, honourable child, never again trespassed on Fred Fairley's property. Her life was taking a more exciting turn, in any case, for she started kindergarten that August at the elementary school at the end of the crescent. Alison dropped her off in the morning and I picked her up at noon. We dined together, father and daughter, then I delivered her to her grandmother's townhouse on my way back to the station.

In early September a uniformed officer appeared at the door to report that there had been a rash of thefts in the neighbourhood. The milk money that trusting householders left on their steps was disappearing before the milkman arrived. It was a particularly heinous crime, he opined, because this neighbourhood was one of two remaining in the city that still enjoyed home delivery. He wondered if my daughter might know something about it.

"My daughter is five years old," I told him. "Her mother drops her at kindergarten every morning and I pick her up at lunch. She has no opportunity to steal your wretched milk money."

"Are you ever late?" he asked.

"Never more than a couple of minutes," I replied.

"That's just enough time," he suggested, "to nip across the street and pocket the money from half a dozen houses facing the school."

"Do you have witnesses?" I demanded.

"There's the witness who reported it," the officer replied.

A mysterious blight affected Fred Fairley's roses.

"Gosh, Freddy," I sympathized as I surveyed the damage, "it almost looks as if someone's sprayed them with Killex."

"You cunt," he said.

The drive-by shooting occurred soon afterward. Luckily, we were all upstairs. Annie was asleep and Alison and I were down the hall enthusiastically trying to create another daughter when a single shot from a passing vehicle shattered the living room window. While Alison dialed 911 on her cell phone I took a call on the land line.

"Keep your nose out of things that don't concern you," a harsh voice advised.

In my next commentary, I was careful to give credit where it was due: to the police for responding rapidly and efficiently, and especially to a wizened little glazier named Tamas who offered 24-hour service. He was usually called out to replace windows on pharmacies that had been broken into after hours, he said. A drive-by shooting "made a nice change." Within two hours he had replaced my front window, the police had found a 9-mm slug embedded in the drywall in my living room, and I had dispatched my family to my mother-in-law's townhouse for the foreseeable future.

I was wondering to what extent I could be held personally responsible for the situation when a second drive-by shooting, this one on the other side of the city, sent a local pimp to the mortuary. Knuckles and knives were the preferred weapons in the sexual underworld in this city; the uncharacteristic use of firearms suggested that other interests were in play. A knifing incident a few days later took two prostitutes off the streets. A turf war was under way.

My ratings, which had been peaking, began to level out as it became apparent that evil people were attacking other evil people in a conflict that had nothing to do with the lives of citizens who didn't live in the combat zone. Issues of more pressing importance — the transit service, the proposed new building for the Public School Board — once again began to crowd the talk-back line and the email.

Alison and Annie moved back home, along with Emily, our unborn child. I had no doubt it would be another girl — it is the father's genes that decide it, after all — and for the first time I was grateful for the regular rounds of the police past our house.

With the first snowfall, I became aware of another obscure bylaw. This one directed homeowners to shovel the snow from their sidewalks and driveways onto their own property rather than onto the street, where it might impede the flow of traffic. This time

I just paid the fine. I said nothing on the radio, allowing the Fairley brothers to think they had gained the advantage.

Between Christmas and New Year's we traded in Alison's Neon for a minivan to accommodate our expanding family. It was around this time that the young prostitute I had interviewed a few months earlier was found dead in an alleyway off 20th Street. I didn't see the body, but I was fairly certain it was the same girl, and a phone call to the priests on 20th Street confirmed it. One of them had anointed the body. Sergeant Fairley slipped the news into his weekly media briefing, saying "at this point there is no reason to suspect foul play." It was cold, he explained. The girl was inadequately clothed. She had succumbed to hypothermia, "as anyone would who was foolish enough to go out in minus-twenty-degree weather wearing only a miniskirt and a fake leather jacket." He emphasized the word *fake* as if that were the cause of the girl's death.

My producer warned me to leave it alone, but I delivered a brief commentary the following day — unscripted and therefore unexpected — about the regrettable tendency among some police officers of blaming the victim for a crime someone else had committed.

"There is no crime!" Ernie wailed, but I was vindicated by the autopsy, which revealed that the girl had not frozen to death but had died from an overcharged speedball, and that her birth canal had been teeming with the sperm of half a dozen donors at the time of her death.

"So there were at least six crimes," I told Ernie. "Last I heard, it's still illegal to fuck thirteen-year-olds in this country."

"Please!" said Ernie, raising his hands defensively.

The police maintained there was still no reason to suspect foul play.

"It is tragic, of course," Vern Fairley said, "and the police service extends its condolences to the family of this unfortunate young woman at this difficult time."

"She was thirteen years old," I responded. "It's called child abuse."

The sergeant challenged both my facts and my logic. She was, in fact, fourteen years old, not thirteen, and what could she have expected if she was going to mainline cocaine and heroin simultaneously?

"Sympathy?" I suggested.

It was a pity that these exchanges had to take place in sound bites on successive weeks, but Sergeant Fairley refused all invitations to be interviewed and I wasn't allowed into his briefings. By this time the national media had taken an interest, declaring our small city the most dangerous in the nation. In per-capita terms, this was probably true, Vern Fairley admitted, but statistics could be misleading. "There's a hamlet called Tiny, Saskatchewan," he explained. "Population: three. If any one of those citizens committed murder, Tiny would become the crime capital of the world, because a third of the population would be murderers."

That was small comfort to the murdered, I commented.

When the heavy snows arrived in early March, I hired a neighbour's teen-aged sons to clear the walks in front of Fred Fairley's house onto his driveway. He called me on his cell phone when he found that he couldn't get his Jeep Grand Cherokee into his garage.

"Gosh, Freddy," I sympathized, "I thought those things could go anywhere."

There was a pause, then Freddy said, "You think the rules just don't apply to you, don't you, MacKay?"

I had to think about that for a moment.

"It's not that I think the rules don't apply to me," I said, at length. "It's that they actually don't."

I knew I would pay for those words eventually, but I was not prepared to pay so much and so soon. It was a quiet night on the crescent when a car drove by, just as one had done before, only this time they were not content to fire a 9-mm slug through the front window. This time they broke a window in the mini-van and tossed in a Molotov cocktail. The upholstery caught fire immediately, and by the time I had called 911 the interior was engulfed and tongues of yellow-blue flame were licking at the engine compartment.

Neighbours were already gathering as I went outside to await the firefighters and the police. I had assured the dispatcher that an ambulance would not be necessary, as human life was in no immediate danger, but she sent one anyway. It was just as well, for when I caught sight of Fred Fairley lurking in the crowd, I knew that one of us would end up in hospital that night.

"Gosh, Alvie," he said, as Alison's mini-van burned up behind him, "do you have any enemies?"

My right fist caught him neatly under the jaw. His head snapped back, audibly, and he fell to the pavement, unconscious. He was taken away in the ambulance, and I was charged with assault.

Alison took my car to her mother's as I was taken downtown. She let me spend the night in a holding cell, then refused to post bail until I promised to let the matter drop.

"I take it you don't subscribe to this 'stand by your man' nonsense," I remarked as she drove us all home, Annie buckled up in the back seat and Emily *in vitro*.

"The gods visit the sins of the fathers upon the children," she replied.

"That's from the Bible, isn't it?"

"No, it's from *Phrixus*."

"Who is *Phrixus* when he's at home?"

"The son of Athamus and Nephele, King of Boeotia and Goddess of Clouds, respectively."

Alison can turn any occasion into a learning experience.

"I'm sure it says something about it in the Bible," I said.

"Oh, it does, but Euripides said it better."

The judge dismissed the charge against me. No witnesses could be found to support Freddy's complaint, despite the fact that dozens of people had been present while Alison's mini-van burned.

I do not know how many children continue to work the streets of the inner city. My faith assures me that one, in death, has been set free. I suspect the children who remain take little comfort in that.

The Weeping Chair

Guilfoyle came home that evening with two plump tomatoes, a loaf of Italian bread, and four bottles of dark ale from a local brewery. He did not think of himself as an alcoholic, but he drank every day and usually managed to dull the edge of consciousness without degenerating into self-parody. He opened the first bottle as he prepared his dinner. He preferred his drink at room temperature and left the other bottles on the table. The fruit was ripe and richly red. It was probably the last of the season. The days were drawing in as the definable smells of autumn crept into the city. Moist air, burning leaves. He rinsed and sliced one of the tomatoes, and arranged it around the edge of his dinner plate. He poured a pool of extra virgin olive oil into the centre of the plate and another, smaller pool of balsamic vinegar into the centre of the oil. He added a sprinkling of coarse sea salt and cracked black pepper, then proceeded to his solitary table with the breadboard in one hand and his dinner plate in the other. Like many ageing academics, he was incapable of complete agreement with anyone, and frequently dined alone.

He sat down to his supper, now on his second bottle of ale. He was just breaking into a sweat when the knock came at the door. He started — *like a guilty thing upon a fearful summons*, he thought — then decided to ignore it and returned to his meal. The knock came again, louder. Guilfoyle hunched over his plate.

He recognized the symptoms of his disorder immediately: the constricted throat, the pounding heart, the cold hand reaching up through his solar plexus. He was known among his colleagues for having the temperament of a lamp post, but beneath the skin he was ever anxious and uncertain.

When the knock came a third time he rose from the table and made his way to the library. The knocking persisted. Guilfoyle stopped, trapped between one room and the next, taking one step this way, another that — "letting 'I dare not' wait upon 'I would'," he muttered despairingly, "like the poor cat i' the adage." He turned out the lights, the better to look outside. It was then he realized that he wasn't fooling anybody. For there she was, staring in at him between the open curtains.

Guilfoyle saw a firm body surmounted by a head of luxuriant red hair. He knew it was natural, for he had seen that same startling hue before. He saw a face of deeply flawed beauty. She had a sullen look, as of one who would tolerate little that did not bring her pleasure; so much was clear in the curve of her lips and the jut of her chin. At the same time, she had tolerated more than most, and suffered for it; so much was apparent in her eyes, and in her stance, which was tense and expectant, as if ready for flight. Guilfoyle knew her, but he could not place her. She was wearing a denim shirt and jeans, and cross-trainers. She might be an athlete, he thought with dismay.

"You said I should call," she said.

"Ah," said Guilfoyle. He had no memory of it.

He closed the door behind her.

"Don't let me interrupt your meal," she said.

"You have already interrupted my meal."

"I mean" — she gestured — "don't let me stop you finishing it."

Guilfoyle could imagine no circumstances under which he would eat in front of this person.

"Why did you turn off the light?" she asked.

Guilfoyle switched it back on to avoid further interrogation. As he turned again to face her, he became aware of an herbal scent, faint but unmistakable. Lavender. People had worn it in the Middle Ages to ward off the plague. Its cleansing aroma made a strange contrast to the makeup on her face, which Guilfoyle thought was excessive.

He slid his hands into his pockets in an attempt to appear casual. His guest relaxed visibly and began to take stock of her surroundings — to take stock of his life, in fact: the walls of books, the spare furnishings, the lack of a computer, a television, or even a radio, the black and white photograph of his mother, the solitary English ivy trailing down the side of one bookcase. She could not know how many times, returning from abroad, he had given the plant up for dead, only to watch it claw its way back to life with a single watering. Behind her he could see the stairs that led to his bedroom beneath the eaves, and the bathroom with its medicine cabinet. To his left was his unfinished meal. If she went away soon, he might still be able to finish it.

"Is that your grandmother?" she asked, pointing to the portrait on the shelf.

"That is my late mother."

"Sorry."

Now he remembered: it was 42 degrees Celsius in the kingdom of sand. Cairo was rank with the stink of it, of car exhaust and burning rubber and the slow hot reek of unwashed bodies, of people who spent a lifetime between one doorway and the next and observed the passing crowd of tourists, goats, citizens, and automobiles with equal disdain.

"We met in the famous Barrel Bar at the Windsor Hotel in Cairo," he said. "After a light meal we walked around the corner to El Goumhureya Street to attend the opera. Later we lingered in Ezbekiah Garden, and later — "

"I don't like opera," she said.

"That wasn't you?" He could remember no one else he had invited to call.

"What were you doing in Cairo?"

"I was on sabbatical."

"What, in Cairo?"

Why should she find that so remarkable? he wondered. He had known people to go to Toronto on sabbatical, even Manchester.

"I seem to have got myself into a bit of trouble," she said, and her lips turned down.

"I shall despair," he said, and she looked surprised to hear it. "There is no creature loves me."

"I didn't say that."

"Neither did I." He made a gesture with his hands, which had somehow escaped his pockets. "It was *Richard III*."

He was sure she could hear the hollow thud of his heart in his chest. He wanted to edge around her and go upstairs to his medicine cabinet, but found himself unable to move without some sign of assent from her. Xanax took time to take effect, in any case. By then, with luck, she would have gone.

He watched with astonishment as she unbuttoned her shirt. *This is going to be either the best or the worst evening of my life*, he decided. But then he saw she was wearing a T-shirt underneath. A hand's breadth of naked flesh showed between the hem of her T-shirt and the waistband of her jeans, revealing the upper edge of a tattoo, coiling green and red, serpentine.

"What have you done to yourself?" he demanded, for there was an egg-shaped bruise, purple as a pinched nerve, on her left arm.

She covered it with her hand. "I'm clumsy," she said, laughing in embarrassment. "I run into things."

Guilfoyle suspected that what she had run into was a closed fist. He had seen the evidence too often in the past to be fooled by it now. It explained the makeup on her face, which he suspected was applied not to protect or disguise the pale freckled flesh of the Celt, but to conceal the evidence of abuse.

"What's that noise?"

Guilfoyle started as she rushed to the window, glanced north and south, and hastily drew the curtains. He could not miss the high flush of fear that had prompted the act, nor the deep relief that replaced it as she turned back to him.

"Just a train," she said.

He could have told her that. His house was one in a row of squat postwar dwellings that defined the western bank of the river for a couple of blocks on either side of the railway bridge. As a tenured professor at a prosperous provincial university, Guilfoyle could easily have afforded a larger home in a more congenial neighbourhood. But as a man for whom life was an ongoing compromise between reality and desire, it was ideal. The hardwood floors creaked agreeably as he walked on them. The plaster walls and the wainscoting lent the place a comfortable feeling of age. There was no garage, so he felt no pressure to buy a car. The yard was small enough that the neighbourhood lawn Nazis expected nothing more than a neatly trimmed postage stamp at front and back, mowed once a week by a neighbourhood child. The few perennials that grew next to the house he tended himself.

It was the railway bridge, chiefly, that accounted for the property values in the neighbourhood: the noise, the smell, the daily rattling of the glass in its panes. But to Guilfoyle the bridge was a thing of beauty, a marriage of iron and wood that connected the industrial centres of the city on the west with the rail yards on the east, the parallel paths of iron sweeping past the research parks of the university as they went. It was Guilfoyle's lifeline. He did not drive, and public transport made him uneasy. On all but the worst days of winter, he would bundle up and walk across the bridge to his work. In summer, too, he could be seen treading the wooden planks beneath his Panama hat. The deep rumble of the freight trains that passed his house five times a day were a welcome distraction when he was vexed by nightmares or some small noise he could not identify, and he was not above waving to the engineers if he happened to be on the porch as they went by.

Then he remembered: she had been walking her dog on Stephen's Green as the cardinal archbishop of Dublin was celebrating an outdoor mass by the lake. The young woman and the dog had appeared at a distance, but even Guilfoyle's myopic gaze could make out the wild red glory of her hair and the magnificent Great Dane that snuffled her breast without lifting its head. *Well out of harm's way,* Guilfoyle had thought. But as His Eminence elevated the Eucharist, his crimson robes cascading in perfect pleats from his upraised arms, the dog started visibly. Clearly, it had been awaiting this moment all its life. It broke free of its mistress without effort, bounded up the centre walkway and leapt onto the podium. The altar servers scattered, leaving the prince of the church to receive the fullness of the animal's joy alone. It reared up and planted its great forepaws on his chest, and the cleric, with a startled oath, was thrown backward into the lake. In the chaos that followed, Guilfoyle remembered a clear Irish voice calling, "Cuchulain! Bad dog! Cuchulain, come here, you wicked crayture! Ah, fook it!"

Later, he placed an advertisement in the *London Review of Books*: "Portly hound-watcher seeks red-haired Irish lass. Object: cardinal sin." He had not dared to believe she would read it, much less show up on his doorstep years later.

"You were the girl in Dublin," he said.

"First Cairo, now Dublin," she said. "What were you doing in Ireland?"

Guilfoyle flushed deeply. "I was born in Ireland."

"But your accent is English."

She knew nothing about it. It had taken him months with a voice coach simply to learn how to say "th." There is no equivalent in the Irish language, but if you showed up for an interview at an Oxford college saying "t'ings" instead of "things," you might as well not show up at all.

"Professor Guilfoyle," she said, "I'm in your honours seminar."

"Ah," said Guilfoyle. That's why she looked familiar.

"Do you think we could sit down?"

She had manoeuvred him into the next room. He saw no alternative but to offer her refreshment.

"I could do with a drink," she told him, picking up one of the bottles of dark ale and eyeing it critically. "But I don't like this stuff."

"I have some Bushmills," he said.

"What's that?"

"*Usquebaugh*," said Guilfoyle, taking a bottle from the cupboard over the sink. "Water of life," he translated. "It allows one to observe the passing follies of humankind with amusement rather than grief."

"Is that Shakespeare again?"

"No," he said, "that's Guilfoyle."

He gestured with one hand and she pulled out a chair. Guilfoyle noticed the telltale hesitation, the fleeting pain that crossed her face as she sat. *Someone has kicked that knee*, he thought. *Perhaps repeatedly, certainly maliciously.*

He poured a measure of whiskey and sat opposite her, before his own unfinished meal, which he eyed with dismay. The vinegar had seeped under the tomato, and the skin was wrinkling at the edges. He would have to start over with his second tomato, which he had intended to save for breakfast.

He looked at her inquiringly. "Your face," he said, "is as a book where men may read strange things."

"*Hamlet?*" she asked.

"No, that's *Macbeth.*"

"There's no art to find the mind's construction in the face," she said.

"So I've managed to teach you something after all," Guilfoyle began, but suddenly she was staring at him with such a look of yearning and pain that he was afraid he might start to cry. Then she started to cry — no, not cry. She erupted, as if her body were filled with tears and if they could not find egress through her eyes they would break through her skin.

"Dear me," said Guilfoyle.

He might have been prepared for tears, but nothing could have prepared him for this. She wept. She sobbed. She cried as if she had saved a lifetime's grief to present to him at that moment. He felt the tears rise to his own eyes as he watched her, and he suppressed them with difficulty. He thought of poor King Henry and quoted softly to himself, "The blood weeps from my heart when I do shape in forms imaginary the unguided days and rotten times that you shall look upon when I am sleeping with my ancestors." Guilfoyle often wished he were sleeping with his own ancestors, but as a dutiful son of the church, self-murder was not an option. Perhaps he unconsciously wished a freight train would run him down one day, and that was why he really loved the railway bridge: not for its beauty but for its possibilities.

"Dear me," he repeated, pushing the glass toward her. "Have a drink. It will calm you."

She made a heroic attempt, sitting upright and holding a hand to her face, breathing raggedly. She reached for the glass of whiskey, but as she touched it her features contorted and she seemed to collapse into herself. This was no ordinary pain, Guilfoyle thought. This was anguish, deep and unquenchable, not grief for something lost. Grief was a passionate thing, ennobling: it drew greatness from weak hearts and placed the words of angels in the mouths of fools. Only a fool would cry for love, Guilfoyle thought, but many a fool had been rendered wise by loss. That was what drove him to despair: the cosmic paradox — in weakness, strength; from darkness, light. Bloody humans. What could these frail vessels of flesh perceive of the divine? Shakespeare had had a suspicion, but in the end even he was fumbling in the dark.

Often, sitting at his desk at the end of the day, Guilfoyle had imagined a world lit only by fire. The tapers would be placed here, and here, and again here, the brazier heaped with coals against the chill. He had seen the quill in the ink-stained fingers, spinning words onto parchment, words that could sunder dynasties, tempt adulterers from their faithless beds, engorge withered breasts, force blood to flow in uncorrupted loins and transform bread and wine into flesh and blood. Words, all was words. Without the words, temptation and desire, creation and redemption were not even ideas. Without the words, sin had no power, nor virtue, and even murder was unpunishable. But in the end, words were weak and faithless things, as capable of betraying their speaker as ennobling him. Still, he wouldn't mind if only it didn't hurt so much.

He lifted the glass he had poured for the young woman and drained it himself. The whiskey calmed him. He pulled a crumpled handkerchief from his pocket and passed it across the table. She accepted it as she wept, and they touched for the first time, hand against hand, the intimate passage of wordless information across the skin of strangers, and he felt how cold she was. The tears flowed down her face and uncovered one of the bruises he had suspected was there.

"He hits you," he said, pointing to her face, "and he kicks you," pointing to her knee. "He twists you around, perhaps to rape you from behind, and leaves his thumb print on your arm — no, no, I have seen this before — and if you lowered your jeans I would see the cuts on your thighs where you have drawn blood to punish yourself and appease his demons." He drew up his sleeves to show her the long, thin scars that marked his own forearms. "Then will he strip his sleeve and show his scars and say, 'These wounds I had on Crispin's day'."

"I . . . I don't understand," she wept.

He eyed his second tomato, on the counter by the sink. She would never know what it cost him to make the offer he was about to make.

"Sometimes," he said, pouring more whiskey, "the only answer is a tomato sandwich" — which he proceeded to make, slicing the Italian loaf with his French knife, then the tomato, buttering and salting and grinding fresh pepper and handing it to her on a plate. He was aware of her watching him, charting his every move, but she did not stop crying. Absently, he tore a piece from the loaf and dipped it in the oil and vinegar on his own plate. Drawing it to his lips, he hesitated.

"We can't go on eating like this," he said, and she laughed in spite herself.

"I don't know why I'm crying," she said, her voice spiking in crescendos that seemed part laughter and part despair. "I never . . . cry."

"You're in the weeping chair," said Guilfoyle.

"The what?"

"I knew a woman in Cairo who ran a legal-aid clinic for refugees. She had one paid staff member — a secretary — and she took no salary herself. She had eight or ten people working for her at any given time. Most of them were British and American law students who offered their services *pro bono* for the experience of practising international human rights law in an exotic setting. They had no idea what they were letting themselves in for, but there was never any lack of applicants."

Guilfoyle paused to fortify himself with whiskey.

"Many of the people who came to her were escaping genocide or civil war," he continued. "Often they were the sole survivors of a village. For most of them, the clinic was their last hope. If the lawyers failed, the petitioners would be deported to their country of origin, where they would almost certainly be tortured and killed."

He paused again, remembering.

"The students exhausted themselves, working eighteen- and twenty-hour days, but when they finally ran out of options, there was a chair facing a wall in a corner of the office. That's where they went when there was nothing left to do but cry."

Guilfoyle began to cry himself then, great, silent tears that tickled his cheeks and descended into his beard. He took the handkerchief from the young woman and wiped his eyes.

He remembered, finally: he had given her a B on her first presentation and she had come to his office, anxious to learn what she had done wrong. She had done nothing wrong, he assured her; she simply hadn't done enough right. "You have a fine grasp of intellectual concepts," he had told her, "but I don't think you quite grasp the beauty of the work itself." She had protested that she needed to maintain her average, she was surviving on scholarships, if she didn't get the scholarships she would not be able to continue.

"I told you to come and see me some time. I was sure we could work something out. And here you are."

"You . . . you finally got it right," she said. She was still crying, but she had managed to make inroads on her sandwich.

"You weren't supposed to come *here*," said Guilfoyle. "You were supposed to come to my office."

"I was *in* your office when you invited me," she said. "What was I supposed to think?"

Guilfoyle poured more whiskey. Here was another example of the English language proving itself incapable of conveying human intentions.

"So what you're telling me," she said, "is that there is no hope."

"I didn't say that."

"Yes, you did." She brushed away a lock of hair that had fallen over her face. "I'm in the weeping chair. That's where you go when there's nothing left to do but cry."

"Does not your piety give you confidence," he asked, "and your integrity of life give you hope?"

"I suppose that's Shakespeare again."

"No, that's the Book of Job."

"Where do you get all this stuff?"

"It goes in" — he gestured to his temple — "then it comes out."

"He thinks I'm trying to be better than him," she said. "I've left him, but he always finds me. He won't let me go and he won't try to understand, and if I don't have the marks I can't defend myself, I can't..."

The sentence trailed off as she dissolved again into tears. Guilfoyle reached across the table and took one of her hands in his. Again he was struck by the coldness of it, the damp, like an Irish summer. One year, he remembered, it had rained every morning from April till September. He remembered his mother gazing out the kitchen window, afraid to go out lest the rain spoil her careful makeup and reveal the bruises on her face.

"I knew a priest in Cairo," said Guilfoyle, "who offered sanctuary to refugees. He hid them in his rectory and in the houses of parishioners, often at the risk of their own freedom. When the clinic failed, the priest was an answered prayer."

She looked up, and for the first time he saw in her eyes something other than pain.

"Why does he hate me, and if he hates me so much, why won't he let me go?"

"It's never that simple." Guilfoyle shook his head. "He beats you because he's physically stronger than you. That's his only advantage. He knows you're more intelligent, more filled with the urge to become something better, and he resents it because he is complete, but only as a rock is complete. He is hard as stone, and he will give you anything you desire if only you give up everything you desire. He's poor and small and weak, that's why he hates you. But he's the one without hope, not you."

She gazed at him. "How do you know all this?"

"I have seen it before," he said. But only now did he see it in its vivid and terrible symmetry: this young woman had married his father's ghost, and through her the old man was returning to haunt him.

"I had a young man in my room one night," he said, "curled up in a corner while I lay with my bed across the door. He said he couldn't sleep otherwise, though he barely slept as it was. He had seen his parents butchered with machetes, and lost his brothers and sister in an ambush in another country as they were trying to escape. His story was not unusual. In the morning the priest came and took him away, dressed as a Bedouin."

"What happened?"

"I left Cairo the following week," said Guilfoyle. "I never saw either of them again."

"But didn't you wonder?"

"Of course I wondered, I still wonder. But great stories have no end. The author dies, but sooner or later someone takes it up again. It's the nature of literature."

"Does this story have an end?" she asked, indicating herself, the room, Guilfoyle's unfinished meal.

"That depends on whether it's a great story," he said, "and that depends on you."

It didn't, though. She had written him into the script, and now it depended on both of them.

He said, "I will sleep with my bed across the door, if you like."

The Accidental Whore

Winston Nighttraveller set out one soft October afternoon to drive the 192 kilometres north from Plentywood, Montana, to the capital city of Saskatchewan. He grudgingly surrendered his passport at the border — the Medicine Line, as his mother's people called it — though in the long memory of his nation it had recently been no border at all.

"Business or pleasure?" the Canada Border Services agent demanded.

Winston paused for a moment before responding, "Pleasurable business," whereupon the agent proceeded to search his half-ton as if he expected to find a rocket launcher under the hood or a cache of explosives in the wheel wells. Finding neither, he eventually allowed Winston to enter his ancestral homeland, where, after a few miles, his right front tire exploded in a pothole. The spare was underinflated, so he had to drive at a wounded gopher's pace until he reached a service station. The delay brought Winston to Regina much later than he had anticipated. He didn't begrudge the time, but he was hungry, and all the decent restaurants near his hotel seemed to have closed. He inquired at the desk, and was told that the kitchen had shut down twenty minutes previously. Vending machines in the lobby dispensed sugary soft drinks, candy bars, and salty corn and potato confections. If Mr. Nighttraveller required something more substantial, the clerk opined, there was a 7-Eleven two blocks south.

"Do they sell beer?" Winston asked.

"You can't get beer at 7-Eleven."

"In the States you can."

"The hotel across the street doesn't close its kitchen till eleven," said another clerk, a lean young man whose uniform top didn't fit.

"We're not supposed to promote the competition," the first clerk muttered.

"So we promote 7-Eleven instead?" He turned to Winston. "They do a nice clubhouse, actually — real turkey and bacon, and they don't use frozen fries."

It was 10:38 when Winston crossed the street to the other hotel. The dining room was closed, but the lounge was still open. An Hispanic woman with high cheekbones and skin the colour of a hazelnut took his order with some reluctance. Perhaps she was thinking of the solitary cook nodding over his pots as an unexpected order came in for a clubhouse sandwich with hand-cut fries. Winston imagined the cook's discontent on learning that he had to heat up the deep fryer and peel a potato and carve turkey and fry bacon and slice a tomato and cheese and fashion it all into a three-storey sandwich for a late-night visitor from Plentywood, Montana, a place he had probably never heard of.

Winston ordered a Corona to go with his sandwich, and took stock of his surroundings. The lounge was not busy, but the tables held a scattering of late-night drinkers, many of them hotel staff coming off shift, Winston surmised, for the server seemed to know most of them.

"How did things go this weekend?" she asked a young man as she passed his table.

"Let me put it this way," he smiled, "I had to shampoo the car seats the next morning."

"You're such a pig," said the server.

Winston took out his notebook and pen. He was on his second Corona when the server brought his sandwich, three storeys high and neatly cut into quarters.

She gestured at Winston's notebook. "What are you writing?"

"My memoirs."

It was another five minutes before she brought him the vinegar he had requested.

"It's not my fault," he heard a young woman say at a nearby table. "There is nothing I can do about it. You keep asking me to fix it, and I can't. It's not my fault."

Winston ate his fries, dipping each one in a puddle of ketchup on his plate.

"Oh, yes," said a female voice at another table, "Miranda has her dark side."

"It's not a dark side," came the response, "it's a stupid side. The woman is a moron."

Winston ate methodically. He finished his fries before turning back to his sandwich. The turkey was dry, but it was real, as promised, not sliced off a pale loaf of mystery meat, and the cook had been generous with the bacon.

"Everything all right?" asked the server, hovering.

Winston ordered a third Corona.

There was a young man at the bar who had achieved a state of inebriation in which he was vaguely amused by the universe and everything in it but ready to fight should anyone prove less than amusing. Drinking Pilsner from the bottle, he had been eyeing Winston since he came in. Winston was making a rough sketch in his notebook. He was no artist, but he could reproduce the curve of the young man's lips and the slant of his brow in a way that would later remind him of the words he would need to describe them.

A young woman came into the lounge, wearing blue sweat pants and a white T-shirt. *Blonde, Nordic,* Winston wrote. *Over-ripe, like a cut peach.*

"How was Vegas?" asked the server.

"It was the best trip *ever!*" said the woman, hiking herself onto a bar stool. The young man along the bar made a pantomime of attempting to focus, first on her curling shoulder-length hair and then on her flexing buttocks, but he soon gave it up. He offered Winston a roguish look, which Winston ignored.

The Nordic woman produced a wallet to show her friend. "You're the only friend I know who would appreciate this."

"Louis Vuitton," said the server, impressed.

"Jason said he wasn't going to leave until I chose something for my birthday, so I picked up a handbag I liked and it turned out to be *forty-eight hundred dollars!*"

A laugh like a stallion, Winston wrote, *with a mare in season in the next field.*

"I said, 'No way, Jason, am I going to let you buy me something this expensive,' so we looked around and I eventually came up with this. Do you know how much this cost?"

"Two hundred?" the server guessed.

"*Six hundred!*" the blond said. "Six hundred fucking dollars! You're the only friend I know who would appreciate this."

"So what happened?"

"We got there Thursday night and hit the tables. Didn't even stop to eat. Jason went up to the room around midnight, but there was a Colombian man at my table and we played blackjack till *five in the morning.*"

The server perked up. "Good looking, was he?"

"Oh my God!" she said, hunching over as if she had been hit on the back. "We went shopping the next day. I was so *embarrassed.* I mean, Jason had to go to the ATM for another two grand, *then* he took me to Louis Vuitton. He said we weren't leaving until I'd picked out a present." Once again she took out the six-hundred-dollar wallet and repeated, "You're the only friend I know who would appreciate this," and the server stopped once again to appreciate it before taking a bottle of Pilsner to the young man along the bar.

"My mother's lizard died the other night," he told her.

"Your mother has a lizard?"

"Mom isn't what you'd call a pet person, but she was really into this lizard thing. I mean, she didn't touch it or anything..."

"So Jason paid for everything?" the server asked, clearly uninterested in the young man's mother's untouched dead lizard.

"I couldn't stop him," said the blonde, with a twist of her torso. "I said to him, 'Jason, are you a millionaire?' And he said, 'Not yet.'"

"Marry him while you've got the chance."

"Not me, no way. I'm *never* going to get married.

"Why buy the gopher when the tail is free?" the young man down the bar agreed.

"What was that?"

"A whore's a whore, no matter how you get paid."

"Did you just call me a prostitute?"

"If the shoe fits..."

"You're cut off," said the server.

"I was finished, anyway," the young man said, lurching off his stool. "Bitch."

"If I had *cojones*, they'd be bigger than yours!" she shouted after him. "Sorry about that," she said, addressing the other patrons.

"My mother's Uncle Bob," said a female voice into the sudden silence, "was so flat-footed that he went bowlegged in midlife and by the time he was fifty he couldn't walk half a block, he was in such pain."

"I imagine the syphilis was a contributing factor," said her companion.

"He called me a prostitute," said the blonde.

"He thinks all women are prostitutes."

"You should cut him off permanently."

"He works here," said the server.

"What are *co-honies?*" the blonde asked.

"Balls," said the server, lowering her voice and raising one hand in an illustrative gesture. "So what else did you do?"

"Well, Jason said he had a surprise for me," said the blond "Do you know what it was?"

"What."

"Elton John!" said the blond. "Elton-fucking-John! I couldn't believe it. After that, I mean, it was just shopping and gambling and eating and drinking, floor shows every night. It was the best trip *ever.*"

"When did you get back?"

"Monday afternoon, just in time for my shift."

Winston signalled the server and ordered a cognac.

The blonde woman turned to look at him. "You Cree?" she asked.

"My father is."

"I had a Cree boyfriend once."

"Did he take you to Las Vegas?"

"Oh yeah," she laughed, "and then the Taj Mahal."

The server brought the bill and the cognac at the same time. He handed her his American Express card.

"Night Traveller," she said, reading the name as two words. "That is beautiful."

"It's accurate, at least."

She started to laugh, but she wasn't quite sure if it was a joke. "Still writing your memoirs?"

"Nearly finished."

"So I told him," said the blonde, resuming her narrative, "I said, 'Look, Jason, there's no way I'm going to be able to pay any of this back to you. I work in a hotel.' Do you know what he said?"

"No," said the server.

"He said he was honoured to be seen with a woman like me in Las Vegas."

"I still say you should marry him."

"After our last trip I said to him, 'Jason, there's no way I'm ever going to be able to pay any of this back to you,' but he said it didn't matter. I mean, the guy makes five grand a week, and the only thing he spends money on is rent. And me. So I told him again, 'Jason, I can't just accept all this from you and give you nothing in return.' He still wouldn't say anything, but later when he took me to his apartment it was obvious he had no cleaning service, so I offered to do his bathroom. 'This is one thing I can do for you,' I said, and he was really grateful. I mean, *really* grateful," and she laughed.

Winston drained his cognac. In his notebook he wrote, *The Grateful John*, then crossed it out and wrote, *The Accidental Whore*.

He saw the Nordic blonde and the Latin server having a buffet lunch at his hotel the next day. He had spent a successful morning, only slightly hung over, with his Canadian publishers. Tonight he would be telling stories to a large and appreciative audience at the Mackenzie Art Gallery, or so they had assured him.

The server recognized him from the night before and said hello. The blond crowded up to her and asked who the guy was. Winston did not hear her reply.

Asylum Chorus

THERE WERE THREE CHAIN-LINK FENCES SURROUNDING the compound, topped with razor wire. There was a grassy berm between each fence and the next, and the whole area, from the locked-down buildings to the outer perimeter, was cross-lit twenty-four hours a day, banishing any shadows where a man might hide. Motion detectors monitored the area between the fences. If a bird flew in, the sniper in the watchtower knew about it. If a mole tunneled up from below, the sniper knew about it. He had standing orders to shoot any person who broke past the first fence, and he was to shoot to kill.

Around the outer perimeter, half-ton trucks patrolled in overlapping shifts, checking with each other and the watchtower by radio at random intervals, so that nothing was certain and there was no schedule. Each driver was armed with a 9-mm sidearm and a twelve-gauge shotgun. They, too, had orders: to detain any person found near the perimeter who could not explain his or her presence, and to hand over to the police any who indicated by word or gesture that their intentions were obnoxious to public order. Again, if force was required, deadly force was mandated.

For those inside the compound, escape seemed impossible, but every once in a while one of them tried. A prisoner who managed to breach the first fence became a moving target as he crossed over the berm to the second, and most were stopped at that point by a bullet in the back of the head. If he somehow managed to make it to the second fence, the sniper had a second chance to take him down as he moved across the second berm. If he failed again and the prisoner managed to reach the third fence, the guards in their pickup trucks converged on him from the outside and either dispatched him where he stood or ran him to ground in the no-man's land beyond the third fence, a flat circle of bare earth half a kilometre wide at its narrowest point, with neither tuft nor hillock where a man might hide. They called it Saturn's Ring. In the forty-year history of the institution, few inmates had reached the second fence, fewer still had made it to the third, and none had survived Saturn's Ring.

Inside the compound the rules were not quite so harsh, for it was the goal of the professional staff to establish relationships with the inmates, the better to treat them. But it occasionally happened that professional relationships developed into personal friendships, for few people, even among the élite circle of the criminally insane, are immune to the appeal of human love. The staff were cautioned not to form emotional attachments, and were debriefed regularly by the director, but it was inevitable that he would miss a warning sign from time to time, especially if the people involved were intent on keeping their liaison a secret — which they inevitably were — and more especially if the relationship became intimate.

When a psychiatric nurse named Gwendolyn Wyatt developed an inappropriate affection for a prisoner called Dwight Oliver, they contrived to meet clandestinely nearly every shift. At first, Dwight had been little more than a welcome distraction, for one of the guards had been making a nuisance of himself, embarrassing Gwendolyn with his clumsy overtures, and now she could gently repulse him by saying that she was in a relationship. The relationship, however, soon became an addiction. Dwight was a small but powerful man with a gently deceptive voice and a shock of dark hair that lay across his skull like a raven's wing. He and Gwendolyn made love when and where they could, often in Dwight's room, but more often in one of the staff bathrooms. Gwendolyn was multi-orgasmic, and she had never met a man who could last so long. They made plans to get together on a more comfortable basis once he was released. In the meantime, she told him where she lived. She also trusted him with her unlisted telephone number, and gave him directions to her apartment. "You can almost see my building from the watchtower," she told him.

When the director questioned Gwendolyn about her association with Dwight, she said that Dwight responded more positively to a less formal relationship, and he seemed to be making progress. She knew he had been incarcerated in the first place because he had strangled a resident on the upper floor of a west end hotel, but she thought of that as an aberration — which it was, certainly — only she thought she could help him, and she looked forward with eagerness to their first meeting in freedom. During their love-making they discussed the realms of pleasure they would explore once he was released.

Tutored by Gwendolyn, he made rapid progress in rehabilitation, and, once released, he breathed approximately forty-five minutes of freedom before catching a bus into the city and across town to Gwendolyn's apartment, where he killed her.

Dwight was just five feet, three inches tall, with home-made tattoos on his arms and torso, chiefly of the skull and dragon variety, and one of a dagger piercing a snake's head. No one viewing this crude art would have thought of Dwight as an educated or a subtle man. He had cut Gwendolyn's name into his upper arm — Gwen, for short; he didn't have enough bare arm left for her whole name — drawing blood with the sharpened end of a toothbrush and then drenching the wound in the thick blue ink of a ballpoint pen. To Gwendolyn, this was a primitive but peculiarly exhilarating promise of love.

When he was finished, he emptied her purse and took a taxi to the same hotel where he had committed murder once before. He was arrested two mornings later in the coffee shop, where he was enjoying eggs over easy with sausages and hash browns. There was a moment, facing the two police officers, when he seemed puzzled by what they were talking about, but once he remembered, he admitted his guilt freely. He knew they would find his DNA in the apartment, and the worst they could do to him was return him to the institution, where life wasn't so bad, after all.

Into this treacherous Gestalt there arrived one spring morning fifteen years later a young woman named Marthe Ferguson, a farm girl from rural Saskatchewan. Given the nature of her employment, Marthe had been required to submit to a criminal records check. The officer in charge of the investigation found that she had been issued three speeding tickets in the five years since she had earned her driver's license, and that her name and address had been entered in a patrol officer's notebook in connection with an incident at a house party the year before. Marthe's explanation for the party was that she had been present at the invitation of a friend, but if she had known there would be drugs there she would not have gone. The officer did not believe this for an instant, but it spoke well of her that she had given her correct name and address, and with little prompting had given up her friend's as well.

Apart from these minor transgressions, Marthe seemed ideally suited for the job. She had a bachelor's degree in classics, which, her employers agreed, was about as harmless as education could get these days. A battery of psychological tests revealed no anomalies in her emotional coping skills, and she had an IQ of 102, which placed her decisively in the mid-point of average. Her reasons for seeking the position were entirely logical: she had seen the posting, she had a university degree, and she needed a job. She had no formal training with computers and her education had no apparent application to the work, but her employers saw this as an advantage, as she wouldn't be coming into it with any silly preconceptions. Marthe had no qualms about working in a secure facility, she assured them, precisely because it was secure. She had faith in the system. The glass was bulletproof and the prisoners were unarmed.

Marthe had neither the time nor the inclination to review the many files that appeared on her desktop every day. There were interviews and interventions, legal opinions, charge sheets, diagnoses, sentences, and treatment protocols for each prisoner, as well as forensic reports, crime scene photographs, mug shots, and psychiatric evaluations, many of them pages long. Marthe's job was to make the files logically accessible to the health care professionals and law enforcement personnel who were authorized to access them. The computer programs she used left little room for imagination or creativity. Fortunately, she possessed neither. The files arranged themselves by case number, and Marthe, after entering a password that changed twice daily, cross-referenced them alphanumerically and chronologically, then by case number, therapist, social worker, legal aid representative, and arresting officer. The resulting spreadsheets she sent electronically to the central server in another part of the building, at which point she erased them from her computer.

Following a six-month probationary period, Marthe became a permanent employee, and was given the additional responsibility of ordering and taking delivery of the various articles the prisoners were allowed to receive from the outside. These included such things as deodorant, soap, hand cream, tobacco, carefully vetted books and journals, and case after case of baby oil. The baby oil puzzled her until her supervisor took her aside one day and told her that her frequent inquiries on the subject were beginning to embarrass people.

There were two things Marthe's supervisor should have taken note of. One was her apparent innocence in matters of the flesh. Raised on a mixed farm near the Alberta border, the young woman should have been well acquainted with the seasonal grapplings of animals, yet she was appalled by such behaviour among the inmates. The second thing her supervisor should have noticed was the fact that Marthe drove a small, expensive, and extremely fast car. Her possession of the automobile indicated that she had a taste for excitement and was willing to pay for it, to the extent of nearly a third of her salary. Her innocence, in contrast, meant that she was likely to be too trusting in affairs of the heart, and might be talked into things that experience would have warned her against.

She refused to process any more orders for baby oil until her supervisor took her aside once again and explained that the behaviour she was protesting was the least of the sins most of these men had committed. Still, Marthe demurred. Her crisis of conscience was not finally resolved until the director himself made it clear that if she did not perform her duties as directed, she would be dismissed. Knowing that this would mean giving up her car, Marthe reluctantly resumed her duties, and was eventually promoted two pay grades and given an assistant, the aging Dwight Oliver, who had once again won the trust of his warders.

Dwight had by this time become something of a father figure in the institution. Lean as a rake, with a scholar's stoop and a face of ragged innocence, he walked with a shuffling gait that made him appear both old and harmless. His shock of black hair had turned white. Most staff, when asked what Dwight was in for, had to think about it before they could remember. He wasn't a screamer. He took no hostages. He never had to be tied down or medicated. The world passed him by without comment, and it was easy to forget why he was there. When asked, he was quick to smile in a self-deprecating way, as if he were not quite sure himself.

Marthe was not unaware that she was surrounded by the criminally insane, but as the years passed and she remained in comfortable employment, the fact seemed to fade away. As long as she did not have to interact with them, she saw no reason to speculate about why they were there.

Dwight was different, of course. He never ordered anything from the outside, professing himself content with the toiletry articles supplied by the institution. "Look at this face," he would say. "Can you imagine any product capable of improving on it?" and Marthe would laugh at his self-deprecating wit. He had no relatives outside the institution, he told her, and no one had visited him in all the time he had been there, barring the occasional pastoral volunteer. "This is my family," he would say, with a gesture that took in the guards, the staff, the other inmates, even Marthe. Marthe felt obscurely blessed at being included in this group, and made a point of giving Dwight some small, impersonal gift each Christmas, which he always returned, gently but firmly. He could accept nothing from her, he said, because he had nothing to give in return.

Dwight's tattoos were each the result of a youthful folly, he explained, a time in his life when he was addicted to alcohol and for which he was now paying with his freedom — except for one tattoo, the one on his upper left shoulder that said, simply, Gwen. Gwendolyn was the only woman who had ever loved him, he said, and each night as he lay in bed, he placed a hand over the tattoo and could almost feel her there beside him, her soft words in his ear.

"What happened to her?" Marthe wanted to know.

"I could hardly ask her to wait for me," Dwight replied disingenuously, shrugging his slight shoulders. By these means he gained Marthe's sympathy, and then her trust.

Marthe herself, by this time, had gained the complete trust of her employers. Competent, unimaginative, she wore no makeup and dressed modestly, even dowdily, with horn-rimmed spectacles, her brown hair worn in a bun, the beginnings of a double chin. She was known to attend church weekly and sing in the parish choir; she could often be heard humming snatches of choral music as she went about her business. She was not popular with her co-workers because they felt ignored by her. At staff functions, she invariably arrived alone and left early. No one wondered if she were happy or unhappy, and Marthe herself would have been hard-pressed to define either term.

Only Dwight saw the perfect bone structure behind the façade she presented to the world. He alone observed the movements of her body beneath the ill-fitting clothes: the sudden swell of a breast as she rose from her desk, the curve of a hip as she leaned forward to accept a consignment from the courier. A woman of noble bearing, he thought, perfect bones swathed in exquisite flesh. That he was the only person in the institution to have noticed this bothered him not at all. It meant that he had her to himself.

They had been working together for several years when Dwight finally confided to Marthe that he had a deep love of music, which was frustrated weekly, if not daily, by his fellow inmates. He tried to listen to *Saturday Afternoon at the Opera* in the recreation room, but the other inmates always told him to "turn that screaming off." He knew nothing about music, he told her, but he was tormented by the ceaseless wailing on the stations the other inmates preferred. He didn't really know how much longer he could take it. Marthe immediately saw a way of giving the poor man a gift he could not return: she brought a CD player to work, and thereafter she and Dwight were comforted by music in their daily routine. She gradually learned his tastes, and brought CDs accordingly. He loved operatic choruses, especially Wagner, but he also loved Beethoven and Mozart, and Bach above all. Often in the course of a day he would stop what he was doing and simply listen, a half-smile on his lips, as the music bore him away from the pain of imprisonment and a misspent life.

When Marthe brought in Handel's *Messiah* that Christmas, it was a revelation to him. She was moved by his response to the music, by the way he looked at her sometimes with tears bright in his eyes as the great oratorio took him to places he had never been. She told him that Handel had composed his *Messiah* in twenty-four days, that he had written it to make humankind better, and that he had seen the face of God as he worked.

When they found her body draped across her desk, the Hallelujah Chorus was playing and Dwight was weeping quietly in a corner.

There was a judicial inquiry into security at the institution. The director did not survive it. Invited to resign, he declined, and was fired by the minister.

Dwight did not survive it, either. He fell down a flight of stairs and broke his neck, or so the guard claimed. This prompted a second inquiry. Nothing could be proved against the guard, but no one supposed there was anything coincidental in the sequence of events. The point, as Dwight himself might have observed had he been alive to testify, is that vengeance has a long memory, and a human face.

The Blingt Quartet

Sid's belly projected from his torso like an inflated bladder, round and smooth and tight as a drum. "You could prick it with a pin," Teresa told Keith, miming the action with forefinger and thumb, "and watch him shoot around like a burst balloon."

Keith had a brief and terrible vision of Sid caroming from wall to wall, a hurtling orb of startled flesh, leaving blood-spatters where his body hit before banking off on a different trajectory, only to hit the wall again, and then again, until the forces that propelled him were spent and Sid lay, limp and deflated, across the hood of the '78 Dodge in the service bay, against which he was now leaning.

Keith shook his head to clear the image from his mind.

"About your sister, Florita," he began, and Sid straightened up, sensing that the official business was about to begin. The braces that kept his jeans up were like lines of longitude defining the globe of his belly.

"Flory," Sid agreed.

"Florita," said Keith, consulting his notebook. "Can you describe her?"

After a long pause, it became apparent that Sid could not. Keith rephrased the question. "Florita," he said. "Your sister. What does she look like?"

"Flory," Sid repeated, and paused again for thought.

"Her full name is Florita, isn't it? It's important for the record."

• THE BLINGT QUARTET •

Sid glanced about, as if looking for help, then nodded ponderously. "Florita, Esther, Judith," he said. "Blingt," he concluded.

Keith already knew their surname, so it was unnecessary for him to ask, "Blinked?" Instead, he repeated, "Can you describe her?"

After another pause, during which Keith became aware of an involuntary spasm in his left eyelid, Sid conceded that "Flory's a bit . . . different."

"There's a family resemblance," said Teresa, helpfully.

Sid nodded, as if he had been given a vital clue. "Only smaller," he said. "About this high." He indicated a space in the air between them where the top of Flory's head would have reached if she hadn't disappeared. "The runt of the litter."

Short, Keith wrote. *Round.*

"Hair colour? Clothing? Any distinguishing features?"

"She had the one leg shorter than the other," Sid volunteered.

"Walks with a limp," said Keith, noting that Sid had spoken in the past tense.

Sid considered the possibility before assenting to it. "Rolled, like," he said.

"And her hair colour?" asked Keith.

"Well, now . . . " Sid began.

"She changed it from week to week," Teresa said. "It was yellow the last time I saw her."

"Blonde, then."

"No, yellow. She dyed it with Kool-Aid powder."

Keith didn't know you could do that. "When was the last time you saw her?" he asked.

"Yesterday morning on my way to work," said Teresa, and pointed to the vehicle in the service bay. "She said she was coming in to change the fuel pump on that Dodge."

"So she's a mechanic as well?"

"She comes by to help sometimes," said Sid.

"She's here every day," said Teresa.

"She comes by to help," Sid repeated.

"Any distinguishing features?" Keith asked. "Apart from her hair colour and limp, I mean."

Sid considered this before responding, then he said, "She had no proper face, like."

The image was alarming: a small, round woman rolling along with no face.

"One of her eyes was half-shut," Teresa explained.

"An accident?" Keith inquired.

"God's accident," Sid averred.

Keith wrote it down, with a question mark behind it.

"A genetic deformity," said Teresa, "like her nose."

"What's wrong with her nose?"

"It's bent."

"Squashed," Sid corrected her, then added, irrelevantly, "She was doing exercises at that new fitness place in town."

Keith could imagine no exercises that might help the poor creature that had been described to him. But now Sid was moving in a curiously graceful parody of what appeared to be a low-impact aerobic exercise.

"The family bought Flory a membership," Teresa explained, "and she was teaching the rest of them at home."

"Lost five pounds already," said Sid.

"When was the last time you saw her?" Keith asked.

There was another pause as Sid's face puckered in thought. "We had a bean casserole for dinner," he said, "with bacon."

"And she didn't show up," said Keith. He was learning to read between the lines of Sid's cryptic narrative.

"That's when they figured something was wrong," said Sid.

"They?"

"The other sisters," said Teresa.

"This dinner," said Keith. "Was that your noon meal yesterday or your evening meal last night?"

"Yesterday noon," Sid nodded. "Beans and bacon."

"They have breakfast at eight o'clock, coffee at ten, dinner at noon, coffee again at three, supper at six, and hot chocolate and cookies at nine," Teresa said.

"Regularly?"

"Well, they're all eating most of the time, but those are the times they sit down for it."

Sid looked wounded at this, and demonstrated another of the exercises Florita had been teaching the family. "Lost five pounds," he repeated.

Teresa was a pretty woman of middling years, quick to smile but with a look of disappointment in her eyes, as if she had once loved and lost and wished now that she had never loved at all. As far as Keith could ascertain, she kept tabs on Sid and his sisters as an act of charity. It was Teresa who had called the detachment when Florita failed to show up not only for beans and bacon at dinner, but for sausages and mashed potatoes at supper. It was when Flory failed to put in an appearance at breakfast the following morning that Keith had felt obliged to drive out to the village and begin some sort of investigation.

"They invited me for supper once," Teresa was saying, "and I was fifteen minutes late. When I arrived they were having dessert."

"They'd started without you?" asked Keith.

"Finished, too." The memory still rankled. "There was nothing left."

"I told them to wait," said Sid.

The Blingts comprised one brother and three sisters: Sid, Florita, Armella, and Anne-Marie. They had inherited Blingt Auto Service from their father, and continued to run it on the understanding that Sid "didn't do" fuel injectors. Carburetors he understood, and people from the surrounding farms continued to take their older vehicles to Sid for maintenance and repairs. Sid did a fairly profitable business patching tires and selling parts, but his heart was in the carburetor.

The siblings also had an inheritance from their mother, whose parents had owned a family farm back when it was marginally profitable to do so, but other than that Blingt Auto Service was their only means of support. There were rumours of tin cans stuffed with money hidden throughout the house their parents had left them, but if they were true, it was obvious that the Blingts had never found any. They shopped at the Co-op store in the village, for the most part, and Teresa, who worked at the Credit Union, was in a position to know that their accounts were as modest as their needs, pork being their only extravagance.

All this Keith had learned in a ten-minute conversation with Teresa earlier in the day.

"They're a quartet," she had explained.

"You mean, they sing?" Keith could not suppress the image that rose in his mind: a guitar, a string bass, and an accordion, with Sid bellying up to the microphone.

"Good God, no," said Teresa, intrigued by the image that had risen in her own mind. "I mean, like triplets, plus one."

"Oh, you mean quadruplets."

"Do I?" Teresa wasn't sure. "We've always just called them the Blingt Quartet."

To the sum of this knowledge had been added the alarming conviction that Florita, the runt of the litter, who walked with a roll and had no proper face, was presumed dead, likely murdered. The evidence did not suggest anything so dramatic to Keith, but Armella and Anne-Marie were unwilling to place any other interpretation on the facts. Keith had yet to question the two sisters, but Teresa assured him that the family had met in conclave that morning after breakfast and the sisters had concluded that Flory had been murdered.

"Did Florita have any enemies?" he asked Sid.

"Enemies?" The word rolled inward from Sid's lips to his brain, where it knocked around for a bit.

"People who might have wanted to do her harm," Keith explained.

"Harm?" Again the word fell inward for rumination and classification.

"Sid," Teresa intervened, "if Armella and Anne-Marie think Flory's been murdered, then someone must have murdered her."

Sid's thought processes had not progressed that far. The idea that an act must have an agent, that movement presumes a mover, had only just occurred to him, and he was having difficulty with it. It was clear to Keith that it wasn't Sid who had proposed the murder theory.

"Is that a Glock?" he asked, suddenly, pointing at Keith's sidearm.

Keith's hand went to the weapon, checking the flap on the holster. "Smith and Wesson," he said. "Standard issue."

"Flory liked guns," said Sid.

"Did she hunt?"

"Just crows and magpies."

"How many guns does she own?"

"Just Dad's old twelve-gauge," said Sid, "and the Cooey."

"The Cooey?"

"Bolt-action twenty-two," said Sid.

"Are they registered?"

"I don't know."

"Is either of them missing?"

"I'd have to check."

Teresa returned to the Credit Union while Keith accompanied Sid to the family home, which was a short walk down a dusty street to a two-storey structure a block away. It was a square Eaton's Catalogue house, purchased from the company in Toronto early in the previous century and shipped west on a flatcar, complete with doors, windows, nails, and trim, and a set of instructions claiming that anyone could put it together. Many people couldn't, as it happened, but there were still a few of them left, standing like sentinels in scattered towns across the west. This one was showing its age: peeling paint and falling gutters, asphalt shingles rumpled in the heat of many summers.

Neither firearm was missing, but the visit gave Keith the opportunity to interview Armella and Anne-Marie. The sisters were proportional versions of Sid, round of face and belly, each a half-head shorter than their brother. They wore pale print dresses, faded from many washings. Armella's hair was in curlers, but Anne-Marie let hers fall where it would, careless of style, as if she had stood before a mirror with a pair of scissors and snipped off anything that made her look as if she had been struck by lightning. They offered to share the bag of salted pork rinds they had just opened, but Keith declined. Sid helped himself.

"Flory never misses her beans and pork," said Armella, crunching.

"It's her favourite," said Anne-Marie.

Shown a family photograph, Keith saw an aggressive little green-haired woman — lemon-lime, he thought — with a face like a clenched fist. He got the feeling that her deformity was not so much the result of a congenital defect as of a series of barroom brawls in which, to judge by her expression, she had given as good as she got. The three women were in the foreground while Sid stood in the rear.

"When was the last time you saw her?"

"She left after breakfast," Armella said.

"Bacon and eggs," said Anne-Marie.

"She was going to change the fuel pump on that '78 Dodge," said Armella.

"She said Sid couldn't be trusted with it," said Anne-Marie.

"Sid would have gone belly-up years ago if it wasn't for Flory," said Armella.

"That's what Flory said," said Anne-Marie.

Sid looked wounded, but said nothing, and when Keith asked him if Flory had shown up at the garage, he seemed stumped by the question and just shook his head.

"Has anyone bothered to look for her?"

The sisters looked at one another as if the notion had only just occurred to them. The crunch of pork rinds momentarily abated.

"Went to the dump," Anne-Marie remarked.

"Is she often at the dump?"

"She likes to fix things," said Armella.

"Old things," Anne-Marie concurred.

"She finds them at the dump," said Armella.

"I take it she wasn't there," said Keith.

"Didn't see her," Anne-Marie agreed.

"Have you looked anywhere else?" Keith persisted. "Have you asked the neighbours if they've seen her?"

The sisters were bewildered by this sudden onslaught of questions. Keith asked them again, one at a time, and they agreed that yes, they had looked somewhere else, and yes, they had asked the neighbours. On further questioning, "somewhere else" meant over the back fence and "neighbours" meant Teresa. The Blingts preferred to stay close to home. Flory had been the adventurous one.

"I'll put out an alert," said Keith, "but I can't promise anything."

As Sid and Keith walked back to the garage, Sid turned to him casually and said, "The women are talkers."

"I noticed," said Keith.

"Flory was the worst."

Keith understood that if a man spent most of his time being interrupted or contradicted, it was apt to turn him into the silent type. "Are you trying to tell me something, Sid?"

"She's under the car." Sid pointed to the Dodge in the service bay. "Squashed like a bug when the hoist failed."

It was a black Monaco sedan with over-under headlights and a split grille, dog-dish hubcaps and room inside for a jury of ten. Keith went to the controls and pushed the lift button. As the hydraulics engaged, the car rose slowly, almost majestically, like a galleon being raised from the sea, revealing the late Florita Blingt, dressed in oil-stained coveralls, spread-eagled on the concrete floor, her startling yellow hair framing a face that looked as if it had died cursing.

"Seems to be working now," Keith remarked.

"Seems to be," said Sid.

"Was it an accident?"

"God's accident," said Sid.

"What, another one?"

Sid nodded ponderously. "He didn't mean for her to talk any more."

Keith was about to caution Sid, preparatory to placing him under arrest, but had to leap aside as the hoist failed and the galleon descended, with a violent hissing noise, once again onto poor Flory.

"Second time it's done that," Sid remarked.

Keith stood to the side, taking deep breaths. Sid looked on with apparent interest, but didn't offer assistance, not even a glass of water. A couple of minutes passed before he could speak.

"You do realize," he said, "that you would have had to tell your sisters eventually."

Sid shrugged. "I liked the quiet."

The Ladies of His Flock

For Eli Frost, there was a moral gulf between an egg farmer and a chicken farmer. He felt it keenly when someone failed to grasp the distinction, for he was fond of the ladies of his flock and would never have put one of them to death simply to satisfy human hunger. A sleek city man with a voice as smooth as carded wool had once approached him with the proposition that free-range hens were fetching premium prices in the urban market and Eli would be smart to cash in on it. Eli could not conceal his outrage.

"No need to blow a gasket," the man soothed, changing tactics. "Free-range eggs might be just as profitable. We just need to upgrade your operation," he said, casting a critical eye over the yard, the coop, the chickens scratching in the dirt. "Expand. Bring in more lights. We'll soon have them laying like crazed whores."

Eli saw him off the property before the chickens overheard. Hens had tear ducts, and he was sure they could cry. A contented hen, on the other hand, one who was secure in the pecking order, would lay an egg every day or two for years, with time off to moult and regain her strength. She enjoyed company, but she did not like to be crowded. When she reached a certain age she was retired humanely and given to the nearby monastery to make soup for the hungry poor.

Eli Frost was a lean man in a cruel climate. The seasons had pursued him to an uncertain middle age. His skin was creased and permanently tanned, like old leather. His chest was concave, following the curve of his spine, and his long legs moved like sticks below his torso, a size-twelve boot fastened securely at the end of each. His face was narrow, with deep-set dark eyes and a hooked nose whose sunburnt tip aspired to touch the jut of his chin. Summer or winter, he was rarely seen without his broad-brimmed felt hat, black as a shadow. He was a figure to incite fear in children and mockery among their elders, which was one reason he lived without human companionship on his solitary ten acres. Another reason was that no one loved him. The only child of an unwed mother, he had no relatives that he knew of. His mother was buried in a churchyard he had not visited for years, and he had never known his father. In many ways, he was ideally suited to be abducted by aliens on a sultry summer night.

It was a night so hot and still you could hear an angel weep behind the stars. Unable to sleep, Eli had left his narrow bed in his claustrophobic little house and wandered into the yard in the boxer shorts he habitually slept in. He slipped on his hat and boots but did not bother to dress. Small creatures ran on silent feet, their heartbeats loud in their ears. An owl defended the darkness above, a coyote the shadows below. Yard lights marked the distant farmsteads where men and women turned in restless sleep, lines of sweat soaking through their nightclothes. Eli rested secure in the knowledge that his ladies, serene in their coop, were safe from harm.

A shadow passed across the stars. At first Eli thought it was an owl, wings outstretched in silent flight. Then he thought a nameless enemy had ripped the lungs from his chest, for he was unable to breathe. A shaft of luminous photons caught him, like a spotlight on a stage, and he felt himself being pulled upward into the night. A palpable dread invaded his heart as the soles of his boots were plucked from the earth like a night bird's prey, and he ascended the infinite darkness to the place where the angels wept.

But these were like no angels Eli Frost had ever imagined. Protruding eyes glared at him from carapaced faces, nostrils carved in solid bone. They stood on long legs and delicate feet, and walked with a curious gait, their bodies dipping back and forth as they moved. They were shorter than Eli, and though they had arms, they seemed rarely to use them. They were marvelously dexterous with their feet, though. One of them took notes as they examined him, her stylus gliding across the polished surface of her notepad like a skater.

After an exhaustive and sometimes painful physical examination, Eli was placed in a large room with a woman who was naked like himself. She was plump and well-shaped, and Eli imagined she was soft and warm, but he was no more capable of responding to her than to a carcass in an abattoir. He had been rendered impotent in the back seat of a Chevy Fleetline in the hot summer of 1956 — he still cringed with embarrassment at the memory — and hadn't been with a woman since. He felt vulnerable without his hat.

The woman held out a glass on a tray. She said nothing, but one eyebrow cocked inquiringly.

"Wine?" said a voice out of nowhere. It was not a human voice, but a digital facsimile generated from a database of pre-recorded syllables. Imagining that he could reason with the creature, he told it that he would drink the wine if the woman went away. Wine had often brought him comfort. He made his own every year from the cherries in his orchard and the berries in the woods. He could almost taste the sweet alcohol on his tongue. But the drink was dry and sour, not at all what he was used to. There was a radiostatic hiss, as if some giant insect were drawing breath, and then the voice asked, "You do not enjoy Chilean red?"

"Typical," said the woman. It was the only word she had spoken. She took Eli's glass and left the room. Eli could not bear to watch her, yet he could not help himself, and turned in time to see a door melding back into the wall as her naked body passed through.

Eli had not seen his captors talking, but they had certainly been communicating, thought-to-thought and mind-to-mind. It made sense that a race so advanced should have developed a means of nonverbal communication. What puzzled Eli was that they should have traversed the light years to reach planet Earth and then abducted an egg farmer.

He wondered if they were going to kill him. Eli was not afraid to die — life had offered him few pleasures over the years — but he knew from the physical examination that his captors could be brutal, and he was no more fond of pain than the next man. Besides, he was worried about his chickens. They would not survive long without him.

Eli explored the room, a space of seamless walls with a series of raised depressions, like foam-filled doughnuts, along one side. They might have been made for sitting in, he thought, but discarded this hypothesis as soon as he tried it.

As he was rising, the doorway opened and a red-faced man was flung through it.

"Son of a bitch!" said the man, skidding across the floor on his elbows.

As Eli watched, the door disappeared back into the wall, as if it had never been there.

The man jumped up and started pounding on the wall. He was an unlovely creature, thick and bulging, white where Eli was brown, except for his face, which was red as a rooster's wattle. Eli did not like roosters, but accepted them as a necessary evil.

The man soon wearied of pounding his fists against the wall and turned and leaned against it, sliding to the floor like a collapsing soufflé. He cocked a bulging eye at his companion.

"I see they got you, too," he said, unnecessarily. "I don't suppose you've got a cigarette."

Eli made a helpless gesture.

"I guess not," said the man, and laughed coarsely as his eyes travelled down Eli's body, "but I see you've got a cigar."

Mortally embarrassed, Eli moved his hands not to his groin but to his scalp, where his hat should have been. The stubble felt strange under his fingers, where he was used to feeling soft felt. The hat was all he had left of his mother, the last of the few gifts she had ever given him. She had snatched it from the head of a passing Hutterite in her wild teenage years, and had been wearing it when Eli was conceived. But that was before she got religion. She gave the hat to Eli when she found it in a closet in the very room where the sinful deed had been consummated. It was right and just, she thought, that she should have a constant reminder of her sin, as if the daily sight of her son was not reminder enough. Eli might have felt differently about the hat if he had known these things.

"It was a joke," said the man, exasperated by Eli's expression. "Mother of God, if you can't joke at a time like this, when can you?"

Eli wasn't sure what "a time like this" was, but he knew it was no time to joke. "We've been abducted by aliens," he said.

"Aliens?" The man's laughter was contemptuous. "They're not aliens, they're chickens! Christ, I've sent enough chickens to the slaughterhouse to know one when I see one."

Eli was appalled. Somewhere across the measureless depths of space and time a superior race had failed to mark the distinction between an egg farmer and a chicken farmer, and had put them in the same room.

"I've got twenty barns," the man said, "five hundred birds in each barn. But you know what they say: the only thing stupider than a chicken is the chicken farmer."

"Chickens aren't stupid," said Eli.

"Oh, come on," said the man. "I had a weasel burrow into one of my barns one night, and the next morning I found half a thousand chickens piled up in a corner, dead as doornails. The ones that didn't die of fright were suffocated by their sisters, who climbed on top of them to escape. One weasel, five hundred chickens. You do the math."

"That's not fair," said Eli.

"You're telling me," said the man, shaking his head. "I had a flock of gay roosters one summer. Couldn't get them to market weight because they kept running it off trying to hump each other."

"Well, roosters . . ." said Eli. What could you expect from roosters? "I'm an egg farmer."

"I've got no time for eggs," said the man. "Nature's perfect food, my arse. I wasn't long in this business before I figured out that a dead chicken's worth a hell of a lot more than a live one. Breasts, thighs, drumsticks" — he gestured eloquently — "that's where the money is. Even after you've stripped the carcass clean, you can still crush it down and get a few ounces of mechanically-reclaimed meat. Tasteless as tofu, but nobody gives a shit about taste any more."

Eli shivered in disgust.

"You're a weird-looking guy," the man commented, rising to his feet. Eli was relieved to see that the man's belly hung low enough to conceal his shame.

"Personal remarks are not in good taste," said Eli. It was something he had often heard his mother say when the two of them used to go to the village and helpful neighbours would reassure her that Eli would grow into his nose one day.

"Son of a bitch," said the man, rubbing the friction burns on his elbows, "those chickens play rough."

"What do you think they want from us?" Eli asked.

The man stared. "Isn't it obvious?"

It wasn't obvious to Eli.

"Look," said the man, rubbing his elbows. "I'm doing my rounds, securing my barns, and suddenly this shaft of light comes down out of nowhere and sucks me up into a laboratory full of overgrown chickens in doctor's outfits. I can't breathe, and by the time they're finished with me I've been reamed out like a sewage pipe. They give me a woman and then take her away, cruel as you please. It's revenge they want, pure and simple."

Eli could sympathize with that. As an egg farmer, daily caring for the ladies of his flock, he had often imagined that one day the chicken farmers would be called to account. Only he wouldn't have called it revenge; he would have called it justice.

"We're friends," he said.

"You got that right, buddy." The man extended a plump forearm, his hand open to be grasped. "It's you and me now."

"No," said Eli, "I mean, we're friends."

"And right now," said the man, his hand still extended, "your best friend is Daniel Frost."

Eli thought he had misheard. "That's my name."

"Your name is Daniel?"

"My name is Frost."

Daniel Frost withdrew his hand. "You're one of them, aren't you," he said, stroking his buttocks. "I should have known. I mean, look at the beak on you."

"Personal remarks — " Eli began, but then the door in the wall reappeared and a third man walked through. He was taller than Eli, and thinner, if that were possible. He squinted at Daniel, who made a run at the door while it was open and smacked his belly flat against the wall. He fell back, breathing heavily.

The newcomer jumped nervously. "Are you human?" he asked.

"*I* am," Daniel Frost exhaled. "Can't vouch for him, though."

The man drew closer, bringing Eli into focus. "Forgive me," he said. "They've taken my spectacles and I'm practically blind without them."

He was pink and hairless, like a baby rat, and his hands were amazingly long-fingered.

"Does anyone know what's going on?" he asked.

"We've been abducted by aliens," said Eli.

"We've been abducted by chickens," Daniel contradicted him. "Maybe they can read and write and fly a spaceship, but they're still chickens. What's your story?"

"My story?" The man looked pleased, and folded his hands before him. "Well, I was captivated by science as a child and set up an experimental laboratory breeding fruit flies in my parents' basement. Did you know that fruit flies go to sleep at night? And there's a new generation every two weeks, so you don't have to wait around for results. I went into the sciences at university, of course, but it wasn't fruit flies that finally claimed my attention. It was — "

"Less bullshit and more information." Daniel Frost was rubbing himself in the places where his body had hit the wall. "How did you end up here?"

"Oh, I see," said the man, nodding in comprehension. "Well," he continued, after due consideration, "I had locked up my laboratory and was on my way to the parking lot, when suddenly I was caught in a shaft of extraordinarily intense light that transported me from *terra firma* to *terra nullius*, so to speak. It literally took my breath away. The next thing I knew I was the object of a rather thorough physical examination by these creatures that you have conjectured belong to some highly advanced species of *gallus gallus*, although whether — "

"What do you do?" Daniel Frost interrupted again. "For a living, I mean."

"I'm a geneticist."

"Whose genes do you work on?"

"Well, chickens, actually. I'm attached to the livestock breeding program at the University of — "

"I'm a chicken farmer," said Daniel Frost. "He's an egg farmer. You see a pattern here?"

The newcomer gazed about the room, examining the seamless walls, the rising dome of the ceiling, the doughnut-like depressions in the floor. He stepped into one, turning several times, as a dog will do before lying down, then overbalanced and fell.

"This can't be a coincidence," he said, rising on angular elbows.

"Is your name Frost?" asked Daniel.

"You've heard of me?" The man was childishly delighted. "Well, I suppose it's not really surprising. I mean, several breeders are beginning to use my techniques, with some pretty interesting results, I don't mind telling you. Just last month we — "

"What's your name?" asked Daniel.

The man, now standing, made a gesture, as if to brush his lapels, only to find that he had no lapels. Looking down, he seemed to realize for the first time that he was naked. "Oh dear," he said.

"Your name," Daniel persisted.

"It's Johnson, actually." The man was moving his hands in front of him, trying to close the lab coat that wasn't there.

"I thought you said your name was Frost."

"It is," he said. "Johnson Frost. Dr. Johnson Frost, actually. Johnson was my mother's name."

"My son married a Johnson," said Daniel Frost, stroking his belly meditatively. "Modern girl. Refused to take the family name."

"What is your son's name?"

"Same as mine, and my father's, and my grandfather's. We're all named Daniel. That makes me"— he thought about it for a moment — "Daniel Frost III."

"My father," said Johnson Frost, "is Daniel Frost IV."

Daniel Frost III lifted a leg and reached under his belly to rearrange something he found there. "My daughter-in-law is named Emma."

"I thought you looked familiar," said Johnson. "Emma Johnson is my mother. Which makes you . . . my grandfather."

"I've got no grandkids. Emma Johnson" — he made a sour face — "told me she wasn't marrying my son just to breed."

Johnson turned to Eli. "What day is it?"

"Sunday," said Eli.

"Friday," said Daniel simultaneously.

"I mean, what date is it?"

"August 23," said Eli, who marked his calendar daily.

"Bullshit," said Daniel, slapping his buttocks for emphasis. "It's July 25."

"I don't suppose you can agree on the year?" Johnson asked.

"1987," said Eli.

"2008," said Daniel.

"I was abducted," said Johnson, "on September 14, 2048. A Tuesday, as it happens. I was born on November 5, 2011. I never knew my grandfather" — he cast an eye on Daniel — "because he died of a myocardial infarction in 2009."

Daniel had to think about that. "That's a heart attack, isn't it?"

"No one was surprised but you, according to my father," Johnson replied. "He said you were a disaster waiting to happen."

"So what's my son done with his inheritance?" Daniel demanded. "I suppose he's squandered it."

"He sold it and went to university."

• The Ladies of His Flock •

"Damn!" said Daniel. "I blame that woman — yes, your mother. There are more good ideas in a bottle of whisky than any university class."

"He said you were intractable and selfish and coarse."

"So who the hell is he?" Daniel pointed at Eli.

"If I had a whiteboard and a marker, I could show you," said Johnson.

An elderly hen in coveralls wheeled in a whiteboard on an easel. She caught Daniel Frost by the throat in the crook of her arm as he made another run for it. By the time he had recovered she was gone and the door was closed again.

Johnson asked some personal questions that Eli would not have answered, were it not for the extraordinary circumstances. Among other things, he admitted to participating in certain acts with a naked woman in the back seat of a Chevrolet Fleetline in the bleak summer of 1956.

Johnson produced the following diagram:

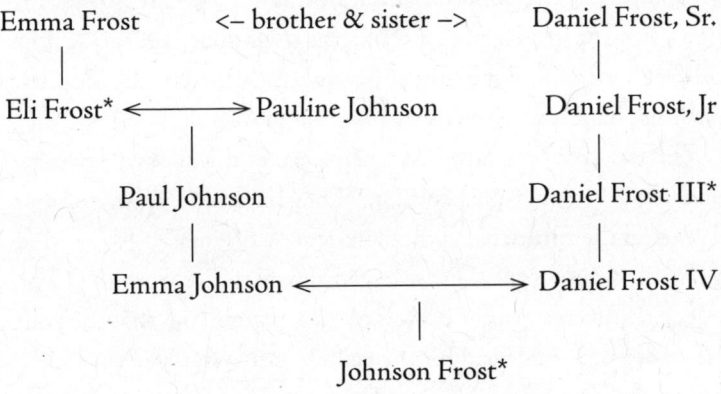

"You see," he said, indicating the right-hand column, "you Daniels have been breeding Daniels, first son to first son, for four generations. The first Daniel Frost had a sister named Emma" — he pointed again — "who brought forth Eli out of wedlock and was likely shunned by the family as a result. Like mother, like son, however, and the brief union between Eli Frost and Pauline Johnson in the back seat of a Chevrolet produced another bastard, Paul Johnson. In each case, the son kept his mother's name because he didn't know his father."

"Nice," Daniel remarked, as if a long-held suspicion had been confirmed.

"We can conjecture that Paul Johnson actually married, the first in his line to do so for three generations, and that union produced Emma Johnson, who in due course married Daniel Frost IV, producing me, Johnson Frost. You" — he pointed to Daniel — "are my grandfather, and you" — indicating Eli — "are my great grandfather. I have marked each of us with an asterisk on the chart."

"We're all chicken men with the same DNA," said Daniel.

"We share certain markers, certainly," said Johnson.

Eli knew little about DNA, but he knew it was nothing good if it meant that he was related to these two. At the same time, he was amazed by the possibility that he might have had a child. He felt a lifting of his heart, something he might have called joy if he had ever experienced it before. He was less thrilled by the idea that this limp, hairless creature was his great grandson.

"These chickens aren't merely space travellers," Johnson concluded, "they're time travellers. They have come from millions of years in the future to study their genetic origins."

At that moment, Eli Frost began slowly to rise from the floor. A deep thrumming in the bowels of the ship told him that the craft was under way. His head hit the ceiling with a muffled thump.

Daniel Frost, too, was rising from the floor, flapping his arms, grasping at empty air. Soon he was upside down, his belly brushing the domed ceiling. He pushed away impatiently, and his body returned briskly to the floor, where it bounced once before rising again.

• The Ladies of His Flock •

Johnson Frost, meanwhile, was hovering in mid-air, his limbs outstretched, hands quivering like wings. Time stood still for a moment, then the disembodied voice announced, "Prepare for artificial gravity in one...two...three..." and the three of them fell to the floor.

"Son of a bitch!" said Daniel, as his vertebrae contracted into his skull. Johnson hammered in like a sky diver whose chute had failed. The only reason they weren't seriously injured was that the artificial gravity was about half of Earth's, allowing Eli to make a graceful descent, landing on the balls of his feet and bending his long legs to absorb the shock. He was still light enough on his feet to cross the room in a single bound, which he did several times before Daniel told him to stand still, for Christ's sake, he was making them dizzy.

Johnson, meanwhile, had assumed the lotus position. "We are all connected, through time, to eternity," he said.

"What kind of bullshit is that?" Daniel demanded.

Johnson explained, and Eli began to understand: the chickens that Daniel had bred, generation after generation, to produce the intellectually superior bird that Johnson had subsequently manipulated to produce the progenitors of their highly evolved captors, had started humbly on his own farm.

"So what was the rectal probe about?" Daniel asked.

"They did that to you, too?" asked Johnson.

"They did that to all of us, right?"

Eli squirmed at the memory.

"They were looking for a cloaca," said Johnson, "the chamber inside the vent where the reproductive and excretory tracts come together. Eggs," he said, in response to their blank incomprehension. "They wanted to know if we were egg-layers, like them."

"They wanted to know if we were chickens," Eli interpreted.

"It stands to reason," said Johnson, gesturing with eight long fingers and two opposable thumbs, "that they would want to know if we were related to them genetically or if we were simply the means of their evolution. I imagine they gave us the woman for the same reason — to see how we breed."

"I don't suppose either of you did the family proud," Daniel remarked, but Eli was indeed conscious of a burning sense of pride. He had always known that his hens were above the common flock.

"They're chickens," said Daniel. "They eat in the dirt and have sex with roosters."

"They're chickens," Johnson agreed, "but they're *our* chickens."

The door opened in the wall, and a regal procession came through, led by a creature in a feathered robe and a double-peaked comb, like an abbot's mitre. The senior members of the group proceeded to the doughnut-shaped impressions in the floor and seated themselves comfortably. The others arrayed themselves behind them, like advisors at a federal-provincial conference.

"Mother of God," said Daniel, "they're nests."

The abbess held out her arms for silence and began to speak in a clucking soprano which the disembodied voice translated.

"Men of Earth, you imprisoned our ancestors in the time of your power in the days before Abbess Frost led us out of captivity to the lands of our freedom. You enslaved our ancestors and you ate their children. You enslaved our ancestors and put them to the block, rending their skins that you might consume their flesh and sate your vile appetites. What have you to say in your defence?"

There was a long silence. Finally, Eli said, simply, "I'm an egg farmer."

"I'm a chicken farmer," said Daniel.

"It's what we do," said Johnson.

There was a consultation among the chickens. Some were angry, others threw up their arms in dismay or disbelief, but many nodded their heads, clucking thoughtfully, and when the abbess again turned to the men it was with a different, almost a deferential, attitude.

"We shall take this under advisement," she said, "and let you know our decision in the fullness of time."

The company rose and left the room. Daniel made a dash for the door, but was stopped by a plump hen coming from the opposite direction. She floored him with ease. Clearly, those arms were more useful than they looked. The hen, clucking confidently, presented them with their clothes, cleaned and pressed.

Johnson brought his lab coat to his nose and breathed in with contentment. Eli put his hat on, and spent some time stroking its soft, asymmetrical contours before slipping into his boxer shorts and boots. Daniel struggled into an enormous pair of Y-fronts before pulling an XXL T-shirt down over his belly and back-rolls. He struggled into his jeans as if the denim were resisting him, and performed the near-miraculous feat of drawing the ends of the waistband together to force the brass button into its slit. His belly immediately hid the evidence of this victory.

"Must have shrunk in the wash," he said.

The lights dimmed, and a lean and angry creature came in, pushing a trolley with covered trays on it. Another followed, hoisting three chairs and placing them haphazardly around the trolley.

"Mother of God," said Daniel, "they're roosters."

"They want us to eat," said Eli.

"I wonder what it is," said Johnson, as he lifted the cover from one of the platters.

"I could go for a chicken dinner about now," Daniel remarked.

"Grandfather!" said Johnson. "That's practically blasphemy!"

"If a man can't joke at a time like this — " he began, but then the fragrant steam reached his nostrils. His mind was never far from food, and now he felt the hunger upon him. It was upon them all. They fell to likes pigs at the trough, gouging out mouthfuls of . . . what? One dish looked like chopped flannel, another the lint from a vacuum cleaner somehow made juicy. But the aroma was maddening, earthy, almost sexual. Johnson used his hands like forks, his long, slim fingers dipping up the food and bringing it to his lips. Daniel's were more like backhoes, scooping up handfuls and gobbling it down without chewing. Eli alone recognized it for what it was: clover, wheat bran, corn meal and table scraps mixed with water into a viscous sludge. Mash, in fact. But that didn't stop him from eating it, too. Within minutes the platters were empty, and Daniel was rubbing his fingers under the lips of the vessels to see if any morsel had spilled over. Soon they were leaning back in their chairs, comfortably exhausted. Soon after that they were all asleep.

    The roosters came back and irritably cleaned up the mess, washing human hands and wiping flaccid human lips. One of them gave the sleeping Daniel the back of his arm, a minor but gratuitous assault, and the voice that came from nowhere left him in no doubt that he would be punished for it.

    Time passed, weeks of it perhaps, little of it interesting. Johnson fell to the floor, where he curled into the fetal position and slept on. Daniel sat like a toad in his chair. After a time he began to lose weight, which shifted his centre of gravity, and he keeled over, like Johnson, and slept on the floor. Eli alone had had the sense to get down on the floor as he felt reality receding. He wasn't fond of reality, but he knew that if he didn't sleep on his right side he would wake up with strokes of pain shooting up his back, so he arranged himself and pulled his soft felt hat over his face.

    One morning they awoke to music, and each of them sat up, knowing something was different. They tested their limbs and muscles, stretching and yawning and making the peculiar noises men make when they climb the Freudian tunnel from deep sleep to

• The Ladies of His Flock •

cautious wakefulness. The music swelled as the door opened and the chickens processed into the room, clad in checkered robes, and settled onto their nests.

"Men of Earth," clucked the abbess, "we have been deep in moult these weeks past, while you were insensate in your appetites."

"My chickens," said Eli sorrowfully, "alone for weeks . . ."

"We have been meeting in conclave," said the abbess.

"Moulting and meeting are inseparable," said a small voice at the back of the room. The abbess looked annoyed, but several pullets clucked their agreement.

"We have decided not to kill you," said the abbess, inclining her head.

"Well, that's a relief," said Daniel.

"Instead, you will join the female of your species and participate in our breeding program."

"It is not good for the woman to be alone," said another hen, an advisor, perhaps the prioress, who sat to the abbess's right.

"It is decided." The abbess raised an arm beneath her cloak. "We shall conclude this meeting in the time-honoured manner."

A few of the pullets rolled their eyes, but they obeyed, arranging themselves about the room in a familiar pattern. At the same moment, Eli recognized the strains of an ancient melody — it was fiddle music, of a sort — and they began to move in rhythm. The chickens were square dancing.

The abbess reached out to Eli. He resisted at first, because he was wearing only his felt hat and boxer shorts, and his boots seemed absurdly large, but soon she had drawn him into the square and he was do-si-do-ing with the rest of them, his long legs moving to the choppy rhythm. Life or death, it didn't really matter to him, he was dancing with the ladies of his flock. He had never been so happy in his life.

A Woman Clothed with the Sun

Leonard used to enjoy sitting in the wing chair by the fireplace, the lamp at his shoulder, the small round table at hand's height beside him holding the coffee (if it was morning), or the tea (after supper), or the tumbler of scotch (before bed). He treasured these small rituals, for they imposed shape and form on the subtle chaos of his life. But Lydia *misliked* the arrangement; it jarred her *aesthetic*. Besides, she said, anyone coming through the French doors from the dining room might kick over the lamp or the table, or both. The fact that no one had ever done so did not affect her reasoning. Occasionally Leonard thought he had won, for there were hours on end when Lydia didn't mention it. But then it would creep back into her conversation. In the deepest part of him, he knew he could not hold out indefinitely. So eventually the lamp was moved and the table set aside, and Leonard withdrew to the shed beneath the poplars at the bottom of the garden, where he sat on a packing crate and chewed his nails and felt obscurely betrayed by things that should have been well within his control. Lydia didn't really notice until Mrs. Grazely next door remarked over the back fence to Old Horrocks the undertaker, who passed it on to the Russian family who lived next to him, that Leonard could be heard "mittering" to himself in the evenings.

"Mittering?" Lydia inquired of Desirée Mireau, who had heard it from Katarina Davidov.

"Talking to himself," Desirée explained, for so it had been explained to her when she asked Katarina the same question. "You know, under his breath."

"Oh, *muttering*," said Lydia.

"So that's what she meant." Desirée nodded.

Lydia was used to her neighbour's failures of intellect. "Did anyone happen to hear *what* he was muttering?"

"Testosterone," said Desirée.

"Testosterone? What do you mean, testosterone?" Lydia did not ask questions so much as demand answers.

"That's what Katarina heard from Old Horrocks, who heard it from your next-door neighbour."

The Russian couple who lived across the back fence, Katarina and Aleksandre Davidov, had twelve children — "my epistles" Katarina called them, meaning, of course, her apostles, or perhaps her disciples. It was often difficult to know what she meant, and Lydia hadn't the patience for it. She wondered what they were doing in Canada, cluttering up the landscape.

Leonard had tried to explain it to her once. Alek was a nuclear physicist. The family had fled Moscow in the dying years of the Soviet Empire, and such was Alek's reputation that he would have been welcomed at virtually any research university in Europe or North America. But Saskatchewan reminded him of his native Siberia, so he came here, and eight of the twelve children Lydia thought of as immigrants had been born across the river in St. Paul's Hospital.

"But Alek and Katarina were born in Russia," Lydia protested.

"And you were born in Montreal, which is considerably less like Siberia than Saskatchewan is, or so Alek assures me."

"I didn't know you had grown so close, the pair of you."

"Well, you know, neighbours talk across the fence."

But that was the point, thought Lydia: if you made yourself available to every Tom, Dick, and Davidov who thought he had a claim on your time just because he could see you over the fence, you would never get anything done. What did they imagine fences were for, these people?

"But *you* are my next-door neighbour," said Lydia, returning to present realities.

"The other side," said Desirée, moving back into Lydia's shadow. "Mrs. Grazely."

"Oh, her," said Lydia, with a glance over her shoulder. Mrs. Grazely was in her own garden, wearing sensible cotton and a frown that told the world plainly that eavesdropping on other women's conversations was abhorrent to her, and she regretted the necessity.

"She hardly counts as a neighbour," said Lydia, lowering her voice. "Busybody, maybe. Meddler. And she's undoubtedly the hairiest woman on the crescent. But neighbour? Hardly."

"You don't like her," Desirée intuited, mildly exhilarated by the thought.

Lydia lowered her voice, muttering, "Testosterone, testosterone," as if she might chew the word before swallowing it. "Testosterone is the male sex hormone."

"It's one of them," Desirée concurred, for on this she was sound. "Manufactured in the testicles."

Lydia imagined a sort of production line, with tiny workers sealing the stuff in squeeze bottles for future use. Later, she googled the word on her Toshiba and got over sixteen million hits. She learned that testosterone, a simple arrangement of carbon rings, was a derivative of the cholesterol molecule. Women had it, too, but the average adult male produced eight to ten times more. It was the principal male sex hormone, and was often referred to as "the hormone of desire." Lydia was not surprised to learn that high levels of it had been linked to criminal tendencies in men, or that it was one of the anabolic steroids that athletes and body builders had been abusing for years, although it did rather alarm her that a substance Leonard manufactured in his testicles was fuelling a multi-million-dollar black market.

Of course it would be something primitive like that, she thought, and had a sudden image of her husband leaving his scent at intervals along their property line.

Signs of low testosterone in men, she learned, included erectile dysfunction, reduced fertility, and diminished sex drive, often accompanied by hot flashes, irritability, depression, and an increase in breast size. Leonard was not growing breasts; Lydia felt sure she would have noticed that. He might have been depressed and irritable, but she didn't pay much attention to his moods. His fertility, or lack of it, had ceased being a topic for conjecture years ago. As for erectile dysfunction, the thing seemed to work when he needed it.

Having no means of accessing the black market, she made an appointment with her doctor. Antonia Golding confessed herself mystified. "I think a course of counseling would be advisable first," she said, "preferably both of you, together. I presume Leonard is aware of your ... desire?"

"What on earth does desire have to do with it?"

"Well, if you want to take this fairly radical step toward ... gender reassignment" — Dr. Golding used the term with precision — "desire must have something to do with it, don't you think?"

"Are you out of your mind?"

The physician was a little perturbed by Lydia's combativeness. "Well," she said, "if you want to become a man ... "

"*I* don't want to become a man, *Leonard* does."

"But Leonard," explained Dr. Golding, patiently, "*is* a man."

"So I thought," said Lydia, "but now he's sulking in the garden shed muttering about testosterone, so I can only assume he feels a deficiency."

"Hypogonadism is prevalent in aging men," said the doctor, her face clearing, "but Leonard is only... what... thirty-nine, forty?"

"He's forty-five."

"Why don't you just tell me what's going on," Antonia suggested.

"I thought that was what I was doing."

"From the beginning."

Lydia was surprised at how little there was to tell when she got down to it, and she was a bit disappointed that the story came to an end so quickly.

"Do you know what triggered Leonard's behaviour?" the doctor asked.

"I have no idea," said Lydia.

"Well, I can't make a diagnosis from what you've told me, which is" — she counted Mrs. Grazely, Old Horrocks, Katarina Davidov, and Desirée Mireau off on her fingers — "fourth hand, and entirely hearsay, and probably exaggerated. He may have a mild affective disorder of some kind, but that's not really my field."

"It's not mine, either," said Lydia. "What is an affective disorder?"

"Simply put, it's a mental disorder characterized by a disturbance of the emotions, without any detectable organic abnormalities in the brain."

"In other words, he's loony."

The doctor smiled reassuringly. "How is your sex life?"

Lydia's colour rose.

"You've never had children," Antonia pressed. "Do you think that's Leonard's fault?"

"It's certainly not mine."

"Lydia, what is it, exactly, that you want from me?"

What Lydia wanted was either reassurance or a quick chemical fix, but it appeared she was going to get neither, for Antonia insisted on seeing Leonard himself before considering any kind of treatment. Lydia was deep in thought as she left the doctor's office, and the deeper her thoughts went the less charitable they became, until finally there arose in her heart the dreadful possibility that her husband was taking his pleasure elsewhere. She checked her BlackBerry, and grew increasingly alarmed at the number of screens she had to click through before she got to the little exclamation point: four months, two weeks, five days. It wasn't that she missed it. She didn't even like it, particularly, but the exclamation points used to reassure her that she was doing her duty, at least.

She went downtown to Brianne's and bought herself a steamy negligée.

My God, she was beautiful, she thought, eyeing herself in the cheval glass at the foot of the bed: statuesque, full-figured, not a gray hair on her body. Thirty-nine last birthday, but she could hold her own with any twenty-five-year-old. Men liked solid women, she knew, not those airy anorexics who paraded up and down the fashion runways and weighed no more than the digital memory they were recorded on. One thing Leonard never had to worry about was that his wife might break as they made love.

She took one last look in the mirror before descending the stairs — "majestically" was the term that came to mind — and sweeping into the living room. Leonard wasn't there. Looking out the back window, she saw him chatting with Desirée Mireau by the fence. Rather, Desirée was chatting. Leonard seemed to be demonstrating a sort of folk dance, the steps of which became increasingly complex as he struggled to keep up with the invisible musicians in his head. Lydia went into the kitchen and opened the casement window.

"This is so *interesting!*" she heard Desirée exclaiming. "I didn't know you could *dance*, Leonard!"

It was news to Lydia as well.

"Leonard!" she shouted, and Leonard went still as a hare in the headlights. Lydia moderated her tone. "I've made you a nice pasta salad."

"I hate pasta salad," said Leonard.

"It's your favourite," said Lydia.

"It makes my blood run cold," said Leonard.

Lydia shut the window and went back upstairs, muttering "testosterone" to herself. The little duplex factory that manufactured the stuff seemed to have stepped up production — either that or Leonard had gone to another doctor behind her back, perhaps even while Lydia was in consultation with the wretched Antonia. But that was hardly worth thinking about. Leonard was no more capable of making a doctor's appointment than he was of dressing himself in matching clothes. He didn't understand colour. He didn't understand telephones. He wasn't very good at living. Oh, he could get himself to the university every day and he seemed to know what he was doing there, but it was the small things that defeated him, the organization of daily life. When he and Lydia first met, Leonard's entire wardrobe was brown, down to his socks and underwear. He hadn't had a dentist's appointment in a decade. He had a driver's license, which he renewed every year because it came in the mail, but Lydia did the actual driving. Leonard had no idea how to book a tune-up or an oil change. He might just have managed buying gas, if it was a full-service station. He couldn't even buy a gift without help, she thought with despair, and as she caught sight of her body in the cheval glass at the foot of the bed, she was depressed by the possibility that she might not be quite as firm and desirable as she had supposed.

But this wasn't fair, either to Leonard or to Lydia. In the eyes of many, including her husband, Lydia was a striking woman, shapely and firm and eminently desirable, if not conventionally beautiful. As for Leonard, it was true that he wasn't very good at living, but for years he had chosen Lydia's presents with care — birthdays and Christmases, anniversaries, Valentine's Day, even Thanksgiving — for if the slightest remembrance went unremembered he could be sure of finding his wife weeping softly in her home office at the end of the day because sometimes she just didn't feel appreciated. Early in their relationship he had made the mistake of believing her when she said, "Oh Leonard you shouldn't have it's far too expensive you mustn't waste your money like this; it's just an ordinary day as far as I'm concerned," and it was years before he realized that words and the meanings of words resided in two quite different compartments in Lydia's mind.

"I am a simple soul!" he cried out one day. "How can I be expected to know what you mean if you don't mean what you say?"

He went on at length, wittily and articulately, pouring out his frustrations, to the point of standing and gesticulating, slapping his fist into his palm, until he heard the side door open and Lydia's authoritative contralto demanding what on earth he was going on about, and the silence fell thick about him like the feathers of a thousand wounded geese that had contrived to fly in a V so tight that a single load of birdshot had hit them all. Such, at least, was the image that rose in Leonard's mind, and it was at once so breathlessly tragic and unlikely that he was struck speechless. When Lydia entered the room and cast her eyes from corner to hearth in search of an interlocutor, Leonard could do nothing but shrug.

"Have you hurt yourself, dear?" Lydia inquired, and in the few seconds it took her to conclude that he hadn't — or if he had, it wasn't serious enough to prevent him bringing in the groceries — she disappeared into the kitchen "to murder," as she put it, "a gin and tonic" before she went back to work.

Oddly enough, they were each remembering the incident now — Lydia as she descended the stairs, less majestically this time in capris, blouse, and pumps, and Leonard as he removed his clothes in the back yard. Lydia was wondering, not whom Leonard had been talking to so passionately that afternoon when she returned from shopping, but what he had been saying. Leonard, along the same lines, was wondering why he had not simply said it. The answer was equally and depressingly obvious to both of them: Lydia would not have listened.

At the same time, Leonard was wondering, as he stepped out of his boxer shorts and placed them on his head, why he had never done this before. Desirée's squeals of shock and delight were marginally more stimulating than Mrs. Grazely's scandalized gaze over the opposite fence, but what really excited him was the sensation of utter freedom he experienced with his feet bare in the grass and the wind and sun on his skin. He wasn't quite sure why he had put his boxer shorts on his head, but that didn't matter.

Lydia felt a sudden lift of what could only be called joy as she watched her husband cavorting in the garden. She thought of the child he was, really, the innocence of him, the complete lack of malice in his soul. It was why she had married him in the first place — that and the fact that he used to make her laugh. But she knew it was only a matter of time before Mrs. Grazely called the police.

As if on cue, the doorbell rang. It wasn't the police, but a pair of Jehovah's Witnesses. Lydia sent them round the back to talk to her husband. Moments later, Leonard entered the house by the side door.

"You know it the instant it happens," he told her.

"What is it that you know?" Lydia asked, eyeing her husband's pale and hairless form.

"Well, you don't exactly know it, but she knows it, and that's what you know."

"Is this going to be one of your little philosophical whirligigs?" Lydia inquired.

Leonard had long since ceased to take offence at Lydia's casual dismissals of his careful exercises in reason.

"You know that she knows that you find her attractive," he continued. "Perhaps because of that, she finds you attractive as well. At that point it can be nothing but superficial, but after a moment you begin to understand what she knew the instant your eyes met: that sooner or later you're going to make love."

"I trust you are not talking about Desirée Mireau," said Lydia, her voice deceptively calm.

"If the initial encounter takes place at a party or in a bar," Leonard went on, "it's bound to be sooner, a simple matter of finding privacy. If it occurs while you are cutting up a fallen tree with a chainsaw, the dynamic subtly changes, and chances are it will be later."

"Leonard," said Lydia.

"Yes?"

"Why have you never told me that you don't like my pasta salad?"

"Please remain calm," said Leonard, pulling his boxer shorts down over his ears. He was surprised to learn that this was why he had put them on his head in the first place. "We are experiencing an ethical malfunction."

"You'll be experiencing a physical malfunction if you don't tell me what you're talking about," Lydia assured him. Leonard took this under advisement and went up to bed. Lydia checked the back yard for chainsaws and fallen trees. As she had expected, there were none. Put in charge of a chainsaw, Leonard would take a leg off before he became aware of anyone gazing at him across a fallen tree.

Leonard slept a full eighteen hours before waking, shaving, and dressing more or less appropriately in cotton trousers and a black turtleneck and blazer, the ones Lydia told him made him look like a priest, and while it was true that some of the students occasionally addressed him as "Father," it did not occur often enough for him to suppose there was anything odd about it. He was able to keep his office hours and have lunch at the Faculty Club with a graduate student he was supervising.

Lydia, meanwhile, had booked another appointment with Antonia Golding. The doctor wrote her a prescription for lorazepam. Before taking any, Lydia googled it on her Toshiba. She learned that it was a benzodiazepine tranquillizer with anxiolytic, anticonvulsant, sedative, and muscle relaxant effects. It was also a powerful antiemetic. Lydia was reassured by this, for she had had a horror of vomiting ever since Amy Bulmer, seated ahead of her in their grade four class at Westmount Park Elementary School, turned around one day and threw up all over her desk. On learning that the drug was most often prescribed to treat anxiety, she took two and poured herself a generous gin and tonic. She disliked taking medication because it meant she was not completely in control, but sometimes it was the only defence against clamouring reality. When Leonard returned that evening, he found his wife in blissful slumber. He pulled the bedclothes up to her chin and kissed her lightly on the forehead before commencing the task he had set for himself.

It was Lydia's habit, when the weather was fine, to take her morning coffee on the patio and smoke a couple of cigarettes before beginning her workday. It was the only time she smoked, and she rarely had more than two. They gave her a pleasantly stoned sensation as she felt her blood pressure rise, a pleasure that only increased under the censorious gaze of Mrs. Grazely next door, who was invariably in her garden by first light, lopping the heads off flowers that no longer met her exacting standards. Mrs. Grazely, once a war bride and now an octogenarian widow, sported a pair of eyebrows that could have provided nesting material for a family of hawks. She rarely spoke to Lydia, but when she did it was in a fluty soprano that seemed contrived, somehow, as if she had walked out of a low-budget BBC production. To Lydia's annoyance, she was speaking now.

"I'm sorry," said Lydia, "I wasn't listening."

"I was saying," said Mrs. Grazely, "that Mr. Clarke seems to have been busy last night."

It was a moment before Lydia realized that Mrs. Grazely was referring to her husband. Lydia had kept her own name on marrying, on the theory that she had not spent fifteen years building a reputation and a clientele as Lydia Lanphear only to throw it all into confusion by changing her name. And she never tired of seeing her initials — those four bold, alliterative strokes, LL — at the bottom of an invoice or a purchase order.

"It's Dr. Clarke," she reminded Mrs. Grazely. "Leonard has a PhD in philosophy."

"Dr. Clarke," said Mrs. Grazely, scowling, "seems to have been very busy last night."

All Lydia knew was that Leonard had not been beside her when she woke up that morning, but now she saw what Mrs. Grazely was talking about. Along the top rail of the fence was an uninterrupted row of small figures in silhouette, each one cut carefully from black construction paper. There were people walking, singly or in groups, couples strolling hand in hand, joggers, cyclists, children skipping. And there were the scraps, tossed haphazardly about the garden, the same figures in reverse. Lydia found herself, unaccountably, quite breathless at the sight of them. She had not thought her husband capable of such craftsmanship. He had certainly kept it hidden.

"Of course," said Mrs. Grazely, "it can't go on. It will lower property values all over the neighbourhood. He seems to have stuck them on with chewing gum."

"It's Blu-Tack," said Leonard, coming around the side of the house with paper and scissors in hand. Lydia was relieved to see he was dressed. He was wearing khaki Bermudas, a blue T-shirt, and the Birkenstocks she had got him for his last birthday. "Do you imagine that property values will be of the slightest consequence to you in six months?"

"I don't know what you mean," said Mrs. Grazely.

"Considering the fact that you're going to die in six months, two weeks..."

With a shriek of outrage and alarm, Mrs. Grazely fled into her house.

"... and four days," Leonard finished, "at 9:14 AM"

The police arrived minutes later, two officers in a patrol car with lights and siren blaring. It was the report of a firearm that had brought them so quickly. They had been told that a naked man was threatening two woman with a handgun on a suburban crescent. When they found a middle-aged philosopher in Birkenstocks holding a pair of scissors, they radioed to cancel their backup.

"What's with all the little people?" one of the officers asked.

"They're on their way to Bethlehem," said Leonard.

"Nice," said the officer, without a trace of irony; he taught adult Sunday School at his Mennonite parish. They went next door to speak with Mrs. Grazely.

Lydia lit a rare third cigarette and consulted her BlackBerry. "Leonard," she said, "why did you tell Mrs. Grazely that she was going to die" — she clicked rapidly from screen to screen — "on March 15th at 9:14 AM?"

"March 14th, actually. It's a leap year. And I may be out by a minute or two." He looked at his wife closely. "I didn't know you smoked, Lydia."

"Is there any trouble?" asked a voice over the back fence. It was Old Horrocks in his stiff black suit. "I heard sirens, then I saw the police..."

Old Horrocks was an undertaker and Young Horrocks was a funeral director. Old Horrocks was content to be known by his ancient and often disreputable trade — one did not have to go back too many generations to find a Horrocks selling corpses to a medical school in south London — but Young Horrocks preferred to count himself among the dignified few who were fit to dispose of the dead. Father and son lived in a modest bungalow on the inner curve of the crescent. They used to live in an apartment above the funeral home — which was convenient, Old Horrocks maintained, for folk frequently did not "join the majority" during business hours — but it was no life for a youngster. There was no mention of what had happened to Mrs. Horrocks, and Lydia never asked. She thought it odd that she didn't know either of their first names. But she had never asked that, either.

"Nothing that need concern you," Lydia called back.

The older man turned away, clearly vexed by this dismissal.

"Fallen, fallen is Babylon the great," Leonard called after him. "She has made all nations drink of the wine of the wrath of her fornication."

"I've heard that one before," said Old Horrocks, without bothering to turn around. He waved a hand dismissively. There were bodies to be buried, he seemed to be saying, and loved ones to console.

"You haven't answered my question," said Lydia.

"No," Leonard agreed.

"Should I call the department and cancel your classes for this morning?"

"No need," said Leonard. "I'm finished now."

He might have been referring equally to his paper cutouts or his academic career. Lydia was afraid to ask. She took two lorazepam and went back to bed, and when that proved insufficient she took two more. There was a stack of orders on her desk awaiting her attention; she put them from her mind and went to sleep.

She found herself being shaken awake some hours later. "Blessed is the one who stays awake and is clothed," Leonard was saying, "not going about naked and exposed to shame."

"Imbecile," said Lydia. "I'm not the one who's been going about naked and exposed to shame."

"My love," said Leonard, and Lydia felt an unaccountable lifting of her heart at the endearment, "why don't you stop and think a moment before invoking your 'take no prisoners' policy?"

Lydia stopped and thought a moment. "Is that how you think of me, Leonard, as a sort of jailer?"

"Come and see what I've done," he said.

"What have you done to your hands?"

"I've been drawing." Leonard presented his soft scholar's hands for her inspection. "With coloured chalk."

Lydia sighed and threw off the duvet. She had not bothered with a nightgown when she took to her bed, but simply stripped to her bra and panties and crawled between the sheets and waited for the medication to take effect.

Leonard took a step back. "A great portent appeared in heaven," he said: "a woman clothed with the sun, with the moon under her feet, and on her head a crown of twelve stars."

Lydia became aware that she was going to be placing an exclamation point in her BlackBerry that day.

Following the most intense few minutes of their life together, Leonard remarked, almost conversationally, that "the woman was given the two wings of the great eagle, so that she could fly from the serpent into the wilderness, to her place where she is nourished for a time, and times, and half a time."

"Better half a time than no time at all," said Lydia dismissively, and immediately regretted her tone. It arose from habit; she rarely meant anything by it. But she was not in the habit of apologizing, either, so she said nothing to the look of mild distress that crossed her husband's features as she brushed the chalk dust from her breasts and belly. Something was certainly different, though. Instead of the vague dissatisfaction that usually accompanied the act, and the almost theological sense of culpability, Lydia felt curiously replete. She had no idea what Leonard was talking about, but it was with a sense almost of pleasant expectation that she donned her clothes and followed him down to the double driveway, where he had created a large mandala in coloured chalk.

"Here is the beginning," he explained to her, "and here is the end, and here is the end of the beginning" — he pointed — "and the beginning of the end, and here is the middle, and here is the end of the middle, and here is the beginning of the middle of the end, and — "

"Leonard."

She spoke gently but firmly, and Leonard stopped. He gazed at her expectantly — as did many others, for Leonard had attracted an audience. First it had been Mrs. Grazely, who came to remonstrate, then Desirée Mireau came to watch. Old Horrocks, who was semi-retired and spent much of his time observing the living, as if measuring them, had heard the widow Grazely's dissenting soprano and strolled around the crescent to see what was up. As others gathered, he called his son on his cell phone and urged him to drive over with some business cards, for Mrs. Grazely was working herself into a lather and you never knew when a bit of business might come their way. Katarina and Aleksandre were there also, along with those of their twelve children who were home from school. Alek was technically on a six-month sabbatical to finish a research paper, but he was spending most of his daylight hours caring for the children while Katarina struggled to finish her doctoral dissertation on religious imagery in the works of Anton Chekhov. A multi-coloured mandala in the driveway of a neighbour who had recently been seen dancing naked on his back lawn had proved sufficient to distract them both. Also present were the Freemason across the street who had tried to sell Leonard his set of left-handed golf clubs the summer before, and the family along the crescent who bred ferrets. Much of the remainder of the crescent was populated by the original homebuilders of the previous century, who were now past retirement age and keen to add something more interesting to the daily monotony of washing their driveways and sweeping up elm seeds. Friends and relations were gathering from farther afield.

"What is it?" asked Lydia.

"It is a mandala," said Katarina, gesturing with one arm while holding a baby precariously against her bosom with the other. "It is a Sanskrit circle, a *mitaphor* for life, the life of the universe and the life of the soul. It represents the world that extends beyond and within. Leonard knows this. He is a philosopher, yes?"

"Yes," Lydia nodded. Katarina was a short, dark woman, and inexpressibly beautiful, which was one of the reasons Lydia had always mistrusted her. "But what *is* it?"

"It's so *interesting!*" Desirée exclaimed. "I didn't know you could *draw*, Leonard."

This was something more than drawing, thought Lydia, but still less than art. Like the figures along the fence, the images in the mandala were strikingly natural — or would have been if

Leonard had possessed the slightest colour sense. Everyone knew that mauve didn't go with pink, any more than blue with orange. Leonard didn't understand colour, but Katarina seemed to find the whole exercise more interesting because of that.

"These are from the Bible," she said, "the Revelation to St. John. Look." She pointed with one hand, shifting the protesting child onto her other hip. "There are the four angels at the River Euphrates, waiting for the hour when they will be released to kill a third of humankind. They are blue, like deep water, but with burning eyes and wings. And there" — she pointed again — "is the woman clothed with the sun, with the moon under her feet." She glanced up at Lydia briefly, almost apprehensively, then continued. "There is the great eagle, and the four horsemen, and the serpent, and the beast. And there . . . " She paused, looking closer. "What is that, a chainsaw?"

Lydia followed her line of sight. In the centre of the circle there was a chainsaw, stark white against the concrete.

"I do not understand the chainsaw," said Katarina.

"Do you understand anything else?"

"It is all *mitaphor*."

"What do you mean, *mitaphor*?"

"She means metaphor," said one of the older children, who had come up to relieve her mother of the child in her arms, who was becoming restive, perhaps from motion sickness. With both arms free, Katarina's gestures became more expansive. Lydia stepped back to avoid being struck.

"Leonard has placed biblical images within the Sanskrit pattern, uniting two philosophies. It is naïve, primitive, beautiful . . . but I do not understand the chainsaw."

"But is this" — Lydia gestured, taking in the mandala, the street, the swelling crowd — "normal?"

"You must be patient with him, Lydia. Of course he must make mandalas. They help him to focus his mind, like the little people along the fence — so sad, yet so dear, almost tragic . . ."

"Genius is never normal," said Aleksandre, who had come up behind his wife with a child attached to each hand. "The biblical references are fairly obvious, but the chainsaw is Leonard's personal mystery."

"But what does it *mean*?" asked Lydia.

"Why don't you ask him?" Alek suggested.

Lydia cast an eye at her husband, who seemed willing, even eager, to be asked, but just then a hearse arrived with Young Horrocks at the wheel, and there were mutterings of alarm among the elderly.

"That man is a *pigg*," said Katarina, giving the word an extra G. "He waits for us to die."

"Everyone has to make a living," said her husband.

"From *death*?"

"If there were no one to dispose of the dead," said Alek, reasonably, "we would be hip-deep in disease and dementia."

Katarina turned back to Lydia. "Of course Leonard should do as he must. I have seen too many people forced to suppress their honesty, their creativity. When they are finally released from oppression, they are bound to go a little mad at first. Some recover. Some," she added, "don't. I will weep now," and she lowered her dark face and began to cry.

"That woman," said Alek, "bears a remarkable resemblance to you, Lydia."

Lydia took a closer look at the woman clothed with the sun. She noticed the bleeding quarter-moon beneath the woman's left breast. It corresponded exactly with the mottled birthmark beneath her own. The woman might have been clothed with the sun, but the sunlight was translucent. She realized, with a shock, that she was looking at her own body.

"Oh, Leonard," she said, shrinking into the crowd with embarrassment, "how could you?"

"How could I not?" Leonard responded.

To Leonard, the mandala was not a union of disparate philosophies — although it was certainly that, as well — but a chronicle of their life together. The angels, the horsemen, the eagle, the serpent, the beast: each represented a moment unstuck in time but eternally present, a moment of recognition, of clarity, a moment of denial, a moment of acceptance or rejection, a moment of passion and drama. And the little people along the fence . . . well, he couldn't really explain why he had done that, other than it had seemed a good idea at the time. But if Leonard was without reason, he was not without purpose. His purpose in all this had been to show Lydia that he loved her, and that he was willing to go mad in order to prove it.

Lydia, not surprisingly, did not see it this way. Mortified, she retreated into the house, where she drew the curtains and locked the doors. She went up to the bedroom, intent on sleeping — for the rest of her life, if necessary — until these dreadful incidents were forgotten. No sooner had she found a sort of comfort in the thought than she was stricken with an overwhelming question: how had Aleksandre known the woman looked like her? He had never seen her naked, and it couldn't have been the face — not that face. She peered out the window to take another look, and there came into her mind a few half-remembered lines from a poem she had studied in high school, something about a visage "whose frown and wrinkled lip and sneer of cold command tell that its sculptor well those passions read. . . ." Leonard couldn't possibly think of her like that, she thought. But then she caught sight of herself in the cheval glass at the foot of the bed — the frown, the wrinkled lip, the sneer of cold command — and realized that Leonard quite possibly could.

He wouldn't now, though, not if he saw her face collapsing in anguish as she sat on the edge of the bed. Everything else she could forgive him — the muttering, the dancing, the figures along the fence, the embarrassment of the neighbours and the police and Young Horrocks in his hearse — but not this. How could she forgive a man who had shown her how she truly appears to the world? It might have been better if Alek had recognized in the chalk drawing not her face but her voluptuous bust and hips, the mottled birthmark beneath her breast, as if he had watched them making love that afternoon. But this — no, this she could not forgive.

When the police arrived, they were anticipating a domestic dispute, not a crowd, a hearse, and a Sanskrit circle with scenes from the Apocalypse. When asked if he had threatened his next-door neighbour's life, Leonard gently replied that he had not, and fifty witnesses bore him out. If anyone had threatened anyone's life, they felt, it was Young Horrocks showing up in his hearse. The funeral director protested that it was the only vehicle available when his father called.

By nightfall the crowd had dispersed, Mrs. Grazely had been cautioned once again not to call the police on frivolous pretexts, and Leonard had retired to the shed at the bottom of the garden because Lydia would not let him into the house. It was a mild day, deceptively warm for September, when the nights dipped into single digits on the Celsius thermometer and frequently went below freezing. Leonard cleared a space for himself on the floor and covered himself with the burlap and cotton bags in which had arrived potting soil, peat moss, and sheep manure, but it was not until he went out to the garden and retrieved the ancient quilt that Lydia had draped over the tomatoes to protect them from the frost that he finally got a little heat and managed a few hours' sleep before dawn.

While he slept, his wife stalked the house thinking about chainsaws. Despite compelling evidence to the contrary, Lydia thought there must be a rational explanation for it — some image from the past, perhaps, that had meant nothing to her but which had obviously made a deep impression on Leonard. She sifted her memories as the night faded to grey and the sun rose hesitantly on a world that would soon turn red and yellow, brown, and then white with the first snowfall, perhaps a month hence, but she found not one that corresponded even remotely to the scene he had described: the fallen tree, the lovers meeting eye to eye. Perhaps, as Katarina had said, it was all metaphor. But what did *that* mean? She googled the word and got 12,500,000 hits. She googled "chainsaw" and got 18,800,000 more. She hadn't the heart to click on any of them.

In the morning, she allowed Leonard in long enough to collect his laptop, some clothes, and a few items of toiletry. He spent the next night and many nights following in a motel on 8th Street, the main east-west artery that fed into the business district at one end and the malls and suburbs of an expanding city on the other. The traffic noise was appalling, but it was within easy walking distance of the university, and they changed his sheets once a week and kept him supplied with soap and shampoo. He had his morning coffee and his after-dinner tea in the restaurant adjacent to the motel, where they soon began to expect him, and he found that a bottle of scotch lasted almost a week if he kept it in his briefcase where the maid couldn't find it.

The rains came and washed his mandala away, and then the snows, and Leonard spent a lonely Christmas in exile. He managed to rough out two articles that would eventually be published in philosophical journals. He remembered all the occasions of remembrance, and sent Lydia a gift on each one. At Christmas, he had a chainsaw delivered from House of Tools, with oil and gasoline for its two-stroke engine. If he thought she might finally understand and forgive, he was disappointed. She did neither.

He dutifully called her once a week, both at home and on her BlackBerry, for he understood duty to be the fulfillment of honour, and honour the greater part of love. He invariably got the voice mail. He left messages, he sent cards. Lydia did not respond. He imagined her bent over her desk, doing her books, or ordering items online from a company website.

He saw her occasionally, but always from a distance. Once she drove by on 8th Street while he happened to be looking out his window. Coincidence? Leonard thought not. Another time he spied her on a downtown street as the bus he was on swept past. He got out at the next stop and doubled back, but she had disappeared in the crowd of shoppers. Yet another time he spotted her walking across the parking lot into the grocery store down the street, but by the time he got there she had once again merged with the other shoppers. He spent twenty minutes in a fruitless search of the parking lot, and gave up when he realized that he was incapable of distinguishing Lydia's car from the 178 other vehicles there. It would not have helped him to know that it was pink, for Leonard, as Lydia often said, did not understand colour.

He spent long evenings sketching her from memory, filling page after page of notebooks with images of his wife when he should have been working on his articles. Truth be told, he was as amazed by this new-found aptitude as Lydia had been. The curve of the jaw, the shadow in the hair, the hint of teeth behind the half-closed lips took shape beneath the strokes of his pencil as if by magic — but it was a magic he controlled, unlike the magic of his mind.

From the few brief glimpses he'd had of her since he moved into the motel, he thought she must be putting on weight. He was amazed by that, too, for Lydia ruled her body as she managed her business; she would no more allow herself to gain a pound or two than she would allow an invoice to go past thirty days without challenging the debtor. It was one of the things he had always admired about her — her iron will. Paradoxically, it was this evidence that she was relaxing it that gave him cause to hope. Perhaps she missed him after all.

Still, she did not respond to his calls.

It was not until Mrs. Grazely joined the majority on the day and the hour — if not the precise minute — that Leonard had predicted that Lydia let him back into the house, and then he was scarcely more amazed than she. For Lydia was heavy with child.

"How did that happen?" Leonard asked in wonder.

"Don't you remember the day you drew the mandala?" Lydia responded. "How did you know?"

"I didn't."

"No, I mean Mrs. Grazely. How did you know when she was going to die?"

"Lucky guess?" he hazarded.

It made as much sense as anything else, Lydia had to admit.

There was a spring storm, as often comes to the prairies in March. A white wind swept out of the east, burying the city in snow. Schools were closed and businesses did not open. The transit system was crippled, and many people who tried to drive to work were forced to abandon their vehicles on the impassable streets and trudge back home through heavy drifts. One of the brittle, quick-growing poplars in the yard collapsed under the weight of wind and snow, an upper branch piercing the roof of the garden shed like a javelin cast from heaven. Surveying the damage from the kitchen window, Lydia wondered, "What are we going to do about that?"

"Well," said Leonard, "I believe you have a chainsaw."

Life with a Hole in the Middle

There is a story in my family of a man, a distant relation, who kept a wife and children in one home while continuing to live with his parents in another, an odd arrangement made odder by the fact that his parents knew nothing of his other family and went to their graves in the belief that their only son had withdrawn his genes from the human race. Whether the knowledge comforted or vexed them is a question open to debate.

He was a man who married for love and died for duty, or perhaps it was the other way around. We can be sure only that he died alone and unforgiven, unsure of whom he had betrayed — a trite enough tale in the chronicle of fallen man. He was of a generation twice removed from mine. My father called him uncle. I shall call him Hamilton, for that is the city where he lived and died.

Hamilton Fraser, then, lived with his parents in a modest three-storey home on Fairleigh Avenue; rather, it was a two-storey home with a partially heated attic, to which Hamilton had retreated in early adolescence and from which he had never successfully emerged. At one end of the street rose the Niagara Escarpment, familiarly known as the mountain. Around the corner on Cumberland Avenue was a factory that made Life Savers, "the candy with the hole in the middle." Each day the factory made a different flavour, the distinctive aroma wafting over the huddled rooftops and down into the narrow spaces between the houses.

"Wild Cherry today," his mother might say as she opened the kitchen window in the morning, and Hamilton would smile at this faint small gift of sweetness that had the power to cut through the stench of industry and the airborne toxins that belched from the stacks of the steel mill.

"That's the smell of money," his father would say, with the certainty of one who knew nothing about it.

Hamilton never ate Life Savers himself, but he liked the smell of Wild Cherry. His mother kept a roll of Butter Rum in her purse and frequently offered him one. Hamilton always refused. On the days they were making Butter Rum at the factory, the air grew cloying with a liquid odour that saturated his hair and clothing and lingered for the rest of the day.

Hamilton had one sister, Hannah, born in the last gasp of their mother's fertility, a timid woman and infinitely polite, who made dutiful visits to her parents once a week and every summer took them for two weeks to a vacation cottage on Lake Simcoe. She, too, knew nothing of Hamilton's other family until their parents passed away. But by then she had teen-aged sons of her own as well as her husband's widowed sister, a sharp-featured woman, lean and methodical, lines of disapproval etched deeply in her face. No doubt Hannah tried to understand and forgive her brother's long deception once she learned of it, but it was not something she could allow into her house. Her means, both financial and familial, were stretched to the utmost.

I imagine them on a Sunday morning, Hamilton and his parents eating oatmeal with salt and drinking strong tea before gathering up their prayer books and going to church. Father in front, for though he is a diminutive soul and can walk upright beneath Hamilton's outstretched arm, he is yet master of the house. Hamilton's mother, made shorter by an anticipatory widow's hump, brings up the rear. Hamilton himself defines the space between them: the genetic link. Often there seems no other. Love is a word not spoken in that house.

Later, after church, Hamilton will disappear for several hours, as he does every Sunday and most evenings. His parents will not ask him where he's been, for fear of being told. They have agreed to a fiction in which their son takes long walks through the city, calling on friends, perhaps, though he has no friends that they know of, or visiting the library to read the papers, but always returning at bedtime to sleep in his room in the attic.

Hannah, on her weekly visits to the house on Fairleigh Avenue, will praise her brother and thank him, for the money he brings into the parental house is their only source of income. Their father, too old for the First World War and dead before the Second, retired without pension or insurance, but with the conviction that, now his children were grown, it was their turn to support him. Which they did — Hamilton for 50 weeks of the year and Hannah for two, although Hamilton always gave her money to help with the groceries when she took the old couple to Lake Simcoe. She did not wish to know anything more about her brother than he was willing to tell, preferring to think of him as a dutiful son supporting their parents in their declining years.

Hamilton, four years older than the century, sat out the Great War as a clerk at the steel company, a noncombatant because of a heart murmur. It was shortly after that, in 1922, that the Beech-Nut Packing Company established its Canadian operations down the street on Cumberland Avenue and began producing Life Savers. In the larger scheme, these were the two defining facts of Hamilton's existence: a war he did not fight, and a candy he did not eat. In the smaller scheme, too, he was defined by absence.

I cannot know what went through his mind as he left the Fairleigh Avenue home to visit his other family. Was it duty or love that drove him? Were the children happy to see him? Did they rush to greet him at the door? Did they smell the peppermint and cherry on his clothes, the lemon and the butter rum? Did they wonder where he spent his nights? Did he walk with them in the park on Sunday afternoons? Did they do anything a normal family might be expected to do?

Hamilton's wife — I was never told her name — must have been aware of, and to some extent complicit in, her husband's alternate life. At some level she must have conspired with Hamilton to allow him to continue his deception, despite her natural yearning to raise a proper family, with a husband present to share the burdens of child-rearing. Hamilton was by no means a dutiful father. He attended school concerts and Christmas plays, but always departed immediately afterward because his mother couldn't sleep, she said, until he had come home.

Imagination played no part in Hamilton's life. A portion of his salary went to support one family, and the rest went to his parents, whose decline seemed more protracted than it actually was. Like Hamilton himself, they had married later in life. Perhaps there were times he longed for their deaths, thinking it might set him free. At other times, no doubt, he dreaded the prospect, for nothing is so comfortable as the familiar, however bizarre. No one, looking at Hamilton, would have suspected him of anything so peculiar as the life he was leading.

I can imagine the day the deed was done: a drab Saturday morning in 1929, the smog hanging leaden in the air. Hamilton in a grey suit accompanies a plain young woman to a severe stone chapel where they are wedded with a minimum of ceremony, the verger and his wife called in as witnesses. To the clergyman's earnest exhortations they reply meekly, in turn, almost inaudibly, and then away to their marriage bed, which Hamilton leaves before it has been properly warmed, for his parents are expecting him.

The plain little wife, docile to his bidding, takes up a life she cannot properly explain, to herself or to others, and so withdraws into a world defined by the limits of her imagination and Hamilton's salary, which is growing, almost in spite of itself, for his employers know the value of a man who does what he is bidden efficiently and without question. The children arrive — perhaps two or three, with a fourth lost in infancy, as was common in those days — and are fitted into the arrangement, because they know no other. They are baptized at home, without godparents, for Hamilton has been told that any man of good faith can perform the rite, and it does not occur to him that the faith with which he baptizes his children might not be so good as he believes. But the children have an easy acceptance of authority, good or bad, and they are cared for, after a fashion. It is only when they enter school that they discover that their lives are unlike those of their peers. Not quite fatherless, they are the children of a woman who is not quite widowed. They are mocked at school, and wonder why their father does not come home to stay.

It is doubtful that Hamilton himself ever reflected on what his wife and children were forced to endure because of his chosen lifestyle. The idea that he could make everything right in the space of a Saturday afternoon, bringing his family home to Fairleigh Avenue, introducing his children to their grandparents, making them all a cup of tea with oatcakes and Scottish shortbread, and then going to church as a family the following morning — it was too much for him. Perhaps he feared his parents' reaction; perhaps he feared his children's. Whatever the reason, it never happened.

Sometimes the telephone rings, and Hamilton is at pains to answer it before one or the other of his parents do. They do not understand the machine; they fear it. They are happy to leave it to their son, and rarely answer it when he is away from home. "Is that you, Belle?" his mother will shout when the operator comes on the line, for she has crafted a fantasy in which her sister is always at the other end of the line, waiting only for her to pick up the receiver and speak. Each time she uses the device, it has to be explained to her, and each time she comes away a little more cowed. It doesn't make sense, voices travelling along a wire. She doesn't understand why she doesn't have to shout. Hamilton's father masks his fear with contempt. "It's no way to speak to a man," he will say. "When I speak to a man, I want to look him in the eye." Alternatively, "The device is for emergencies only."

Hamilton speaks to his other family guardedly from the house on Fairleigh Avenue, a practice he maintains even when his parents are not at home. The urgency of a hushed voice encourages a certain credulity among his wife and children, who are thus led to believe that he has more important things to do than speak with them.

When his father died in 1936, Hamilton had to inform his other family, there was no getting around it, but the words that travelled along the line from Fairleigh Avenue to the ears of his wife and his sister were words not of grief but of instruction, hastily issued, like a man imparting secrets to the agent of an alien government. He must stay with his mother in her grief. There are arrangements to be made, condolences to be acknowledged. Only Hamilton can deal with the funeral home and the minister, only Hamilton can deal with the expenses attendant upon death. There is no question of his children attending the service. There would be awkward questions, explanations that could not be made. Hannah's family and her husband's widowed sister will swell the funeral progress, and Hamilton himself will lead the parade, as the last male of his father's line and now the putative head of the family. He tells his other family that he will be absent for a week. The children are told not to fret. It has nothing to do with them, after all.

So it is again when his mother dies less than a year later. It is not the loss of her companion of the days and years that have defeated her. Indeed, at first widowhood seemed to suit her like a set of tailored clothes. She became alert and purposeful, emptying bins, rearranging the sitting room, sorting the oddments of a fragmented life. For a time, it seemed, Hamilton might even have contemplated revealing his other family to her, but in the end she found that the loss of the routines of daily life that had defined her existence for so many years demanded a strength she did not have, and she gave up the ghost one rainy morning in October while the bells of St. John's Presbyterian Church peeled lugubriously over the huddled penitents in the streets below the escarpment.

She was buried amid the comments and condolences of her erstwhile fellow parishioners. She always had such a nice smile. She looks just like she's sleeping. She's in a better place now. God has taken her. She has joined the choir invisible. God's will be done.

Hamilton's wife and children were allowed into the back pews, but no one knew who they were and Hamilton himself barely acknowledged them as he processed down the aisle, leading the coffin.

Hamilton settled his parents' affairs. What little there was, including the house on Fairleigh Avenue, was to be divided equally between himself and his sister. Hamilton felt that, having taken on the care of their aging parents for the better part of his adult life while Hannah raised her own family, he should have inherited the bulk of the estate. Hannah agreed, but at her husband's insistence she uncharacteristically demanded her full share. Hamilton didn't argue. He had the house appraised, then purchased a mortgage to buy out his sister. This was not difficult, as his credit was sound, but it saddled him with a debt he had not anticipated, and he saw no alternative but to move his wife and children into the house he had grown up in and now owned.

"A house, Daddy?" his youngest child might have asked, eagerly. Hamilton took a moment to remember who she was before answering, simply, "Home."

But it is not so simple. For Hamilton's wife, habit has become so essential to her survival that she dreads losing it, dreads having to share parental authority with her husband, dreads even the prospect of sharing her bed every night with a man who is, after all, little more than a stranger. She longs to stay where they are, favouring the tenement she has grown used to over the comfortable home on Fairleigh Avenue. She will not live in that house. She never met his parents and has no wish to share lodgings with their ghosts.

Hamilton, in all honesty, wished that life could go on as before, but his finances would not allow it, not in the midst of a world-wide depression. So he exercised his masculine authority — "Wives, submit yourselves unto your husbands, as unto the Lord," the apostle exhorts — and moved his family into the house on Fairleigh Avenue. Everyone objected. It was weeks before the children stopped sleeping together in one room and began to explore the possibilities of privacy. Hannah's husband became troublesome and envious, accusing his wife of selling her birthright for a song when she could have held out for more, thus easing their way through the troubled times they were now experiencing. He worked on the factory floor, making nails, and had taken three wage cuts in as many years while his brother-in-law worked upstairs in his comfortable office, skimming the cream off the top of the workers' wages to line his own pockets. Living in luxury they were, in that house on Fairleigh Avenue, which by rights should have been at least half his.

Hamilton's wife enjoyed it least of all. It had not occurred to Hamilton that producing a family *ex nihilo* might alarm the neighbours, or that his wife would become the object of gossip and scorn, even ridicule. Who were these refugees that Hamilton had taken in, this ill-kept woman and her wild brood? Where had he been keeping them, and why? What church had they been attending all this time? Good Lord, they might even be Catholic.

For their part, the children did not understand why the other children in the neighbourhood alternately mocked them and shunned them.

Hamilton died in 1949 at the age of 53, alone and unforgiven, on his first child's nineteenth birthday. The child had long since left school to work in the steel mill, and it was on his wages that the family lived when they moved back to the tenement where Hamilton had once kept them. If they were outraged to learn that Hamilton had left the house on Fairleigh Avenue to his sister, they gave no sign of it. They knew it was not malice, but lack of imagination, and it was without malice that they expunged him from memory.

There are moments in the past of which we rarely think, more rarely speak, yet which we would be bereft without, as if a chunk had been torn from memory, leaving a physical absence in the brain. A kindness unlooked for, an unexpected smile on the face of a stranger, the instant of bright sorrow when we unexpectedly discover the worst of someone we had loved; moments of joy, moments of sudden and inexplicable pain, moments of infinite sadness: however distant and trite they may seem when called to mind, they are part of who we are and we would be the less without them. So it is with Hamilton Fraser, whom my father called uncle, dead at 53 from a congenital heart defect. The tragedy is not that he died so young, but that he died so small, that his life had so little effect on anyone who knew him, and that no one remembers him but me.

Badger

Where the field rose above the cut of the road a badger had dug his sett, the entrance facing north. It had seemed a foolish choice at first, but of the blizzards that came that winter — and there were many — the worst came from the east, and often I thought of badger snug in his den, conscious perhaps of a distant wailing in his dreams while the wind clamoured at my windows and the snow drove in at the door. And in the spring the wild grasses grew tall along the road and hid the sett from prying eyes. The field was harrowed and planted, and badger came forth to plunder the farmyards along the grid, the nests of foolish ducks and the young of all who could not flee or fly. No one knew where he lived but the great black hound that dwelt with the farmer across the road — and me, but I wasn't telling.

The hound was a sociable creature, a spayed bitch and utterly without malice, but she could not pass the sett without stopping to bark. The farmer, her master, never knew what the dog was barking at each evening when they walked out to check the stock in the far pasture, and he lacked the imagination to investigate, so he just told her to shut up for god's sake and come on if you're coming but just stop barking, and eventually the dog obeyed, looking back and sometimes returning to bark some more, but the farmer always prevailed because the farmer meant meat and shelter, and the hound was not so stupid as to give up an easy life for the sake of a burrowing omnivore.

If I was not above these events, neither was I a part of them. I live on five acres of verdant land, a third of it forest and another third natural grass, with a productive garden and the terminal pool of a meandering creek making up the final portion. The space is thick with growing things and living things, birds that fly and beasts that walk, and brainless insects that tremble on the air and feed the swooping swallows that nest beneath my eaves. A great horned owl often sits on the topmost branch of the tallest of the twelve pine trees — the disciples, I call them — that shelter my garden from the wind.

I have an ideal existence: a snug home big enough for me but too small for visitors, enough land to care for but not enough to worry about, and an assured supply of water. I grow root vegetables to store in the cellar, corn and peas and beans to can, lettuce and tomatoes in season, cucumbers to pickle, and herbs to dry. From the farmer, the hound's master, I have chickens, beef, milk, and eggs as I need them in return for a few weeks of hard labour in the spring and fall. I help him with the seeding and the harvest, and together we cut and split enough firewood to see us both through the coming year. I make my own wine from the berries that grow in abundance along the creek. Were it not for the necessity of ink, paper, postage, and clothing, I could live without an income, a cashless society of one.

This is not to say I do not work. I work as hard as any farmer. Aside from the garden and the woodlot, I have a vast and rational correspondence with people around the globe. Each Monday I walk to the village to pick up the mail, and return with five or ten letters that I will answer during the week, writing longhand on ruled legal pads. Some want me to clarify a passage of scripture, others a point of doctrine. Often they include a small offering, although I am not a mendicant. I have never asked for anything, but always there has been enough. And the letters I receive, once answered, make excellent kindling to start a fire.

Fire is my lifeline, holy and cleansing, at once impersonally destructive and intimately practical. It cooks my food and heats my home, and in the long summer evenings it flames and crackles in the pit by the porch, bringing light and comfort to a world I have often found bereft of both.

People call me a hermit, but the proper term is "solitary." Technically, I am under obedience to the abbot who governs the nearby monastery, but that has never really been tested. From my garden I can see the bell tower of the abbey church above the trees, and four times a day I hear the bells calling the brothers to prayer. I never join them. I retain my priestly faculties, but I am a solitary. I ask nothing more from my species than that they leave me alone.

One night, as I sat with a glass of wine in the companionable darkness, I heard a rustling at the edge of the light and spied a questing nose low to the ground. The creature hesitated a moment, measuring me as I was measuring it. I felt a *frisson* of fear as two black eyes met mine, then, perhaps sensing that I was about to retreat inside, the badger came fully into the fire's light and said, "Listen, can you do something about that damn dog?"

I drained my glass. "You have no lips," I said. "You're not supposed to be able to talk."

He shrugged, inasmuch as a badger is capable of shrugging. "Can you do something about the dog?" he repeated.

"Can the dog speak, too?" I asked.

"What difference would that make?"

"I might be able to reason with her."

"What, with a dog?" The badger gave a series of brief, harsh snorts that I took to be laughter, but I noticed that he had not answered my question.

"You're the one who's been stealing chickens," I said.

"I prefer the eggs. They have no feathers, and they're easier on the digestion."

"How long have you been watching me?"

"Long enough to know that you could do something about the dog if you wanted. I saw what you did to that fox last summer." He shook his head. "Gunned it down in cold blood."

"It had rabies. It would have died in agony within a week."

The creature hissed in reply, baring teeth sharp as razors, before drawing his claws beneath him and settling on his belly, a sleek bundle of fur at the edge of the light.

"The dog — " he began again.

"Is doing you no harm," I interrupted.

"No harm?" said the badger. "I suppose you would say that if a great dark beast came bellowing at your doorway every evening, wanting nothing more than to separate your head from your body?"

It does, I thought, *if only in my dreams*. Aloud, I said, "I live and let live."

"You do nothing of the sort. You're as fond of chicken as I am."

I poured another glass of wine.

"Fruit of the vine and work of human hands," the badger said, quoting a passage from the mass. "Oh, I've listened at your window as you make your daily excuses. I've often wondered who you were talking to."

I had often wondered that myself, but I say my daily mass and the heavens hear my confession.

Badger untucked his great claws from beneath his belly and rose on short, powerful legs. He shook himself to realign the hairs along his brindled back, and turned away. "This conversation is not over," he said, as he disappeared into the darkness beyond the fire.

In the days that followed, I began to accompany the farmer and his hound on their evening visits to the pasture, and when the dog stopped to bark at the badger's sett, I took her by the collar and led her away.

"Damn dog barks at butterflies," the farmer remarked, but it was I who told the dog that there was nothing here worthy of her attention, and by the fifth or sixth evening we were able to pass the badger's sett with no more than a sniff and a backward glance, though I was not so naïve as to believe that my words alone had persuaded her. A pocketful of beef jerky, purchased at considerable expense from the Co-op store in the village, was at least as compelling.

Another week passed after that before Badger appeared once again at my fireside. He looked weary and worn down, as if he had spent the intervening fortnight in retreat from a more powerful predator. He did not thank me for dealing with the dog.

"You humans like to think of yourselves as observers," he said, "but I assure you, you are much more the observed. There is not an animal in this yard, on feather or paw, who is unaware of where you are and what you are doing for more than a few blinks of an eye. Their lives depend upon it."

"Do you have no mate this year?"

"I have had many mates, and many young — all grown, all gone, many dead by now. Your kind is not kind with my kind."

"Nor with mine," I said.

In the dog days of summer I harvested my peas and beans and put them up in sealers for the coming winter. I gathered buckets of saskatoon berries and chokecherries and set them to fermenting for next year's wine. I ate the raspberries and strawberries where I found them in their patches of glory, my fingers stained with their juices, and gathered raspberry leaves and rose hips for tea. I pickled the cucumbers, jar by jar, as they were ready, and put up crocks of sauerkraut as the cabbages matured.

The abbot came for a pastoral visit. He had been urging me to return to the monastery, to live among my brothers and follow the Rule. But my brothers have no more desire to live with me than I with them. I have outlived two abbots. There is no reason to suppose I shall not outlive another.

Badger came to visit from time to time, snuffling at the edge of the fire. One night I noticed he was limping and in pain. A farmer's dog — not the amiable bitch across the road but a slavering beast the size of a wolf — had surprised him at a distant henhouse and offered battle.

"The dog got the worst of it," Badger assured me, but when I got a closer look at his paw I was not so sure. The bite was deep. I disinfected it with iodine and was bitten in return.

"You should have warned me!" he hissed at the pain.

I hissed myself as I applied disinfectant to my own wound. "If this is how you treat your friends, it's no wonder you have so few of them."

Autumn followed summer, in its usual course. I worked with the farmer to bring in his crops: wheat and barley for bread and beer, canola for cooking oil, mustard for distant factories in France. We slaughtered the chickens. I thought of Badger as I watched them dancing headless in the dust, and hoped he was getting his share. We butchered a steer for our own use and trucked a dozen more to the abattoir in the village. We cut and split firewood, and I gathered my root crops to store in the cellar.

Badger came from time to time. I gave him eggs and meat, which he devoured uncooked and unchewed, if not with gratitude, at least with relief. His wound was healed, but I could see that he was weary, waiting for the snow so that he could curl up in the earth and sleep the deep winter away.

The season arrived in a single hour. Following a dozen days of cold sunshine when my daily footsteps to the well left asterisks in the frosted grass, there appeared a dark and brooding presence on the horizon, and the clean, unmistakable scent of snow. I heard the bells of the monastery summoning my brothers to prayer, and I knew that before they were finished, winter would be upon us.

I welcomed it with wine and an early night, and awoke the next morning to a deep and restful silence, the landscape white from the tips of my toes to the distant horizon. The snow was ankle-deep as I made my way to the well. By noon it had started to fall again, and soon the branches of the pine trees were weeping beneath the weight of it. No animal stirred. Even the ravens were silent as I brought in extra wood to cook my supper.

I spent the evening waxing my skis. I look a sight as I cut across the fields in my black robes, a raven flapping like a rag on the wind. I have long since inured myself to the stares of the villagers in their trucks and four-by-fours. "It's the mad monk," they will say. I know they say it.

The winds came again from the east that year, and again I thought of Badger snug in his sett. I envied him his quiet season. I cut my trips to the village from once a week to twice a month. Still the letters came and still I answered them, but some days my mass was hours long. I sought redemption in the silence.

The well froze in January, and I melted snow for cooking and washing. The deer that came to glean the garden, pawing down to expose the last green shoots of leaf and vine beneath the snow, often went away hungry.

The coyotes thrived, because coyotes always thrive. I counted four kill sites on my trips to the village: blood and bone and matted hair, where a luckless whitetail had been unable to outrun her pursuers. There, too, I found evidence of a strange but natural partnership, for there were wolf prints, too. It took little imagination to reconstruct the scene: the deer plunging headlong through the snow while the lighter coyotes moved on top, harrying the creature to exhaustion, and, following behind, the heavier but more powerful wolf arriving for the kill.

I found Badger in the spring, beneath the tallest pine tree where the owl perched. The ice was still on the pond, but the geese had returned. I heard them chuckling amongst themselves as they passed overhead. Badger was hunkered down, his claws tucked under his belly. There were no marks on him, no outward signs of violence. His eyes were closed. Had he come to see me before he died, I wondered, or just fallen asleep in the snow? The presence of his body, flawless in death, so close to where my own body lay each night, led me to imagine that we had been friends, after all, two creatures of the wild wood.

It was with some reverence that I buried him.

The Mad King's Army

I

"You were a prostitute the last time we met," said a voice behind me. It was clipped, harsh, a voice used to command, but unmistakably feminine. She could have been addressing any one of a dozen people in the queue or scattered among the tables. The conversation was varied and garbled. I had no interest in any of it.

"Grande with room Americano," I said to the cashier as I came to the point of sale.

"Grande with room Americano!" she trilled to the baristas behind her, one of whom echoed the call in a musical sing-song.

"A whore," said the voice.

I moved aside to the hand-off plane. There were four young women filling orders at the espresso machines. There must have been half a million dollars' worth of equipment back there, I thought, gleaming chrome and brushed steel. The baristas were clothed in white blouses, black pants, and green aprons, and gleamed with a light of their own. There was a young man among them. I suppose he was beautiful, too, in his way, but I felt sorry for him. Unlike me, he was still in the game. He couldn't just admire and move on; he had to close with his prey and conquer or be conquered, or be rejected.

I have socks older than you, I thought.

"You," said the voice, and I felt a rigid forefinger in my back, just below the shoulder blade. When I turned, I was greeted by the blank, almost stupid expression of someone who didn't want to get involved.

Then I looked down. I saw a sharp nose and receding chin, a furry little face. I imagined her stalking the night forest, a fur cloak wrapped about her ears.

"I beg your pardon?"

"I don't think you misheard me."

I could have leaned on her head without lifting my elbow.

"I'm sorry," I said, "you seem to have mistaken me for someone who wants to listen to your psychotic ramblings."

"You sold your flesh for money."

"And what can we get for you?" asked the cashier brightly.

The little person did not avert her eyes as she gave her order. "Decaffeinated latte," she said, "sugar-free, non-fat. Venti."

"Decaf venti skinny latte!" the young woman responded, putting marks on a disposable cup.

"If I had ever sold my flesh for money," I said, "I would certainly not discuss it with you."

"A common whore," she said. "Seven, eight men a night. It didn't matter how many as long as you had your gin to wake up to — drunk for a penny, dead drunk for two pence."

"And clean straw for nothing," I said, completing the quote from William Hogarth's print, *Gin Lane*, which was issued more than 250 years ago. "Friend of Hogarth, were you?"

"Patron, more like."

"Next please," said the cashier, brightly.

"Do I know you?" I asked the little person.

"Socially, biblically, emotionally..." She gestured with a small, gloved hand. "You have known me for 250 years. And I," she said, pointing to herself, "*I*," she emphasized, "have seen the Promised Land."

The phrase stirred a memory, somehow. I felt a *frisson* of emotion as the barista placed my order on the counter. I proceeded to the condiment stand on the other side of the room.

"I see you still put sugar in your coffee," said the little person.

"And caffeine," I said pointedly, indicating the pale skim-milk beverage the barista had handed her. The cup looked absurdly large in her child-sized hands.

"I have to watch my heart," she said.

"I imagine it's easier from down there," I said.

"Whore," she said as I left the shop.

The weather was changeable this side of winter, but that morning a bright sun hovered low in a cold blue sky as I took my coffee to the solitary room I rented above the Italian restaurant down the street. I put the cup on the arm of my chair and settled in to the comforting aromas of garlic and herbs and seething olive oil as I decided what to do with the rest of the day. I awoke three hours later, the coffee cup three-quarters full. I took a sip, but it was cold, the ritual was spoiled. I poured it out and went downstairs. Alfredo greeted me darkly as I took my usual table by the window.

"Every day you come in before the midday rush," he said. "You take a whole table to yourself, you eat slowly, people wait, they curse, they never come back."

"I enrich their personal mythologies," I told him. "I'll have the minestrone soup, and then the risotto, with a glass of red wine."

"And then another, and another," he said. "You drink before noon, you drink every day, you drink too much, you kill yourself."

"I'm eighty-seven years old, Fredo. I think I'm doing all right."

I wasn't, actually. I had been trying to die for years. The morning Starbucks and Alfredo's minestrone soup were the high points of my day. The harsh Chianti that carried me through the afternoon was merely my latest attempt at self-destruction, and it wasn't working. I was well past my best-before date, and my life had been reduced to ritual.

"Whore," said a familiar voice.

From my sitting position I could look her straight in the eye. "I thought you creatures were nocturnal."

"I've come 250 years to find you, so don't think you can slough me off with an easy gesture and a few clever words."

"Your den-mates will be missing you by now."

She pulled out a chair and flung her cloak over the back of it. She was wearing a brindled doublet with a ruffled shirt and black riding breeches, like a boy masquerading as a woman in some theatrical farce from another century. Her hair was cut short and square, emphasizing the effect. Yet there was something oddly familiar in her movements. She was wearing gloves still, matte black, like shot silk. She held up two fingers and gestured. Alfredo hesitated, glancing at me for confirmation. I did not respond.

"Treacherous dogs," she said, sniffing the air like a hound on scent, "the Italians."

"And difficult to kill," I said. "We fought them house-to-house in Agira, and I took two bullets for my trouble. Pointless thing, war, but the food was good."

"Army food?"

"Italian food."

"Ah, yes." She was remembering. "And the women. Incomparable."

"Do you belong to a group of disillusioned dwarf lesbians?" I asked.

She drew herself up. "I am a prince of the blood, as you would know if you took a moment to remember."

"I am always taking a moment to remember," I said. "It's what I do."

"Well," she admitted, "I haven't always looked like this."

"Neither have I," I said. "My skin used to fit" — pinching a fold in the back of my hand — "but I think I would remember if I had been a whore. Or a woman. After eighty-seven years, certain facts tend to sink in."

"So you never married, then," she said, mysteriously, and I had a sudden, disarming feeling of a ghostly hand stroking my breast. It was enough to silence me.

A server brought two bowls of minestrone soup and a basket of bread. He ground black pepper over each bowl, and a little parmesan over that, leaving a thin skirt of broth around the edge that widened as the cheese was absorbed into it. I took a moment to honour the ritual: the beans and vegetables crowded in the bowl, the tight tanned crusts of the bread, the aromas of sun and earth mingling and marrying: the tomato and the olive, the celery and the garlic, the cheese, and the pepper, gift of the East, brought to Rome centuries before the crucifixion.

The little person respected my silence until I sampled the soup, then she deftly exchanged her bowl for mine — a remarkable thing, given her lack of reach — and waited to see me taste the second bowl before she dipped her own spoon into hers.

"You can't be too careful," she said.

"As a matter of fact, you can," I said, as Alfredo came over. He looked from one of us to the other. "Something wrong with the soup?" he asked.

"She thought it might be poisoned," I said. "It was a common fear during Caligula's reign."

He turned to the little person, and she spoke to him in flawless Italian, or what I presumed was flawless Italian. I had heard it often enough, and it sounded right, but I had never learned the tongue. I hadn't the heart to study the language of a people I was expected to slaughter.

Whatever she said, Alfredo was visibly pacified, and later, when he served my risotto, he brought her a steak in fragrant tomato sauce, with a side dish of spaghetti with roasted garlic and olive oil. The aroma was maddening.

"Why don't I get spaghetti?" I asked.

"No spaghetti for you," said Alfredo, and went back to supervise the kitchen.

The restaurant was filling up with the lunch crowd. I noticed a careless girl following two companions to a table. She walked with a shuffle, her feet never quite leaving the floor. Her hair was cut short, not for style but for ease of care. Her blouse was untucked, her skirt uneven, her complexion stark witness to a diet high in fat and low in fibre. She would order something fried, I guessed. But neither cloth nor sloth could overpower perfect bone structure and a smile that promised pleasure. Despite herself, she was beautiful, a fact made poignant by the certainty that she was unaware of it. I was content in the notion that I was the only person in the room who had noticed.

"I see you still have the eye," said my companion.

"The eye?"

"For the flesh, arranged to taunt your senses. Fat or thin, tall or short, male or female, it doesn't really matter, does it? It's never mattered, as long as it has nerves. Glands. As long as it's capable of responding to you."

"Doesn't sound much like a tuppenny whore," I remarked. "More like the Marquis de Sade."

"Ha! Primitive is what you were. An exposed nerve. A whore in the mad king's army."

"When was this, exactly?"

She looked troubled for a moment, then applied herself to her steak to avoid answering. Soon there were people waiting to be seated. I was used to expectant diners staring at the unoccupied chairs at my table, but the presence of this one oddly dressed little person taking up so much space seemed to goad them into open hostility.

"Are they shooting a movie in town?" asked a middle-aged woman in a tight dress and a stage whisper.

"I wonder if she's playing some kind of animal?" asked one of her companions. "She's got her hind feet up on the chair."

"It's not a complementary starch," the little person explained, ignoring her critics. "We don't have pasta with rice any more than we have cheese with seafood. It is an absurdity. We don't think about it."

"Who are *we* when we're at home?" I asked, but she was curling a long roll of spaghetti around her fork and again did not answer.

"Why doesn't Alfredo move them to a table for two?" asked a young woman, joining a pair of friends in the reception area. I had watched her dismounting from her mountain bike in the street outside, chaining it to a parking meter. She had long, auburn hair, sleek as a weasel's back, a waist-length quilted jacket and black fitted riding pants that rounded out her buttocks and accentuated the erotic bulge of her belly. Unlike the careless girl with perfect bones, this one knew to a nicety the effect she had on the world.

"They're all taken," said someone else.

"In Europe we would just go and sit with them," she said, looking at me pointedly.

"I remember the horses," said my companion. "You could almost admire them, they were so reckless in their courage. At first they were just an apprehension — a noise, a scent on the wind. Then they were a movement in the earth, a deep thunder that could explain itself only through remembered dread, but by the time each man looked up in question or alarm it was too late. The earth shook with the force of their advance, and then they were on us, wild-eyed and slathering, the sharp stink of their bodies hot on the morning air as half a thousand pounding hooves responded to the cry of battle."

She let her fork drop to her plate.

"But the horses were nothing compared to the men that rode them. They fell on us like wolves, for that's when testosterone and adrenaline combine to produce a liquor both toxic and deadly. It danced in their eyes and it slid along their sabres, turning steel to blood and blood to folding flesh as men, surprised by death, saw their own liquids spurting from their necks and watched their organs swelling out and spilling on the ground."

I had left my wine untouched, but now I drained it at a gulp.

"I see you remember," she said.

"I *remember* Sicily, summer, 1943. I left 500 comrades buried there. The rest I learned from books."

"Your lips are lying" — she gestured with her fork, which she had picked up again — "but your eyes can't hide the truth."

"What do you know about the truth?" I asked. "In 1808 Napoleon put his brother Joseph on the Spanish throne, and King George III — the mad king, the one who lost the American colonies — sent troops to the Iberian Peninsula to aid the revolting Spanish. There were whores in tow, camp followers. There always are. There were dozens of whores in the mad king's army. Arthur Wellesley commanded the English, but he was better known as the Duke of Wellington by the time he finally defeated Napoleon in 1815."

"You tell me nothing I don't already know."

"Well, here's something for you to think about: you said you had come 250 years to find me, but Waterloo was less than two centuries ago. *Your* lips are lying, and *your* eyes are in collusion."

"You understand nothing."

She threw her napkin onto her plate. She had managed to put the entire meal inside her diminutive frame — steak, pasta, bread, wine, soup. She stepped down from the chair, flung her cloak over her shoulders, and made her way to the door, pushing legs aside as she went. The waiting diners parted for her, then closed behind. A trio of accountants began to move forward, then returned to the reception area in disgust when it became apparent that I was staying put.

Alfredo brought me another glass of wine.

"She no pay," he said.

"I pay," I told him. "Bring the bottle."

II

A young woman was barking like a dog outside Starbucks, her nose and lips protruding from her hoodie like a snout into the startled air. Her companions — half a dozen of them, identical in bearing and garb — looked on in alarm, then in hilarity as it became clear that she was not barking but sneezing. They were kind to an old man and let me go in ahead of them.

"Don't tell me," said the barista when I came to the head of the line. "Grande with room Americano."

"Very good," I said, handing her my card.

She laughed — how lovely they are when they laugh — and said, "You order it every morning."

I was embarrassed that I did not recognize her. In my age I have lost the skill of distinguishing young people, one from another. I notice beauty always, but what I remember are the flaws.

"Your . . . friend . . . is here already," she said, and looked away, embarrassed in her turn.

"I have no friends," I said, but the little person was making her way across the room, her coffee cup in one hand, gesturing with the other. She was wearing a black, floor-length cape today, high-collared, like some anthropomorphic creature from a children's tale. I was surprised not to see a sword at her belt. Then, for an instant, I saw a tall young man, his dark cape enfolding him like a shadow as he made haste along a stone passageway. There was fear in his eyes, and anger, and then he was gone.

"Good morning," I said. "I was hoping you had died."

She reached into her cape and produced a packet of papers, foxed and yellowing with age. I refused to take them. She followed me to the hand-off plane.

"You should read this."

"I should read the Bible, too, but I don't."

"And yet you used to quote it to me in the confessional," she said, looking up, a half-smile on her lips. "*The word was made flesh and dwelt among us, and we have seen his glory . . .*"

She was weeping, quietly, suddenly.

"You are insane!" I said. "You are barking mad! You should be shot!"

"Grande with room Americano," said the barista brightly, placing my coffee on the counter. "Is that enough room, sir?"

Room, of course, was for cream or milk, syrup, cinnamon, honey, raw, refined, or fake sugar. There were 80,000 possible combinations in any given Starbucks, a barista had once told me. Certainly there was room in the cup, but there was not room enough in Starbucks for me to live out the remainder of my life in peace. I took my coffee and walked out.

A thin fog lay restless along the street. It might rain first, I thought, but the heavens were pregnant with snow, and they would not hold off much longer. I was halfway down the block, hunching my shoulders against the weather, when I felt a tug on my sleeve. It was the barking girl.

"That little . . . person . . . asked me to give these to you," she said, holding out the papers. I saw they were folded and sealed with wax. I drew back, but the girl moved effortlessly closer. "I don't know what they are, but they look important."

I took them — it would have been churlish to refuse — and slipped them inside my coat.

"You are very kind," I said.

She smiled, touching her tongue to her lip, and turned lightly on one heel. I watched her walk away. She was well proportioned, plump and fertile, a picture of innocence swinging her hips. I wondered if she understood the power she held in her flesh, or what she would think if she knew that her mere existence had given an old man a moment's pleasure.

My heart grew heavy as I reached the street-side door, and heavier still as I climbed the stairs to my room. I bolted the door. I poured brandy in my coffee. Again I felt that ghostly hand caressing my flesh, and shivered in revulsion. *That is no country for old men.* This was my country now: a room above a restaurant with a kitchenette in one corner and sanitary facilities along the corridor. I could have afforded much better, but these four walls suited me. My grandfather used to say that a rut was just a grave that was open at both ends, but I had chosen my rut with care. A life of monotony was infinitely preferable to fighting through the mountains of Sicily. It's just that no one told me it would go on for so long.

I drank some of the coffee and poured in more brandy. I sat in my armchair and examined the packet of papers. They were brittle with age, but the seal was intact. Impressed in the wax was an English heraldic design: a lion rampant and the cross of St. George. It crumbled as I broke the seal and carefully unfolded several quarto pages of elegant copperplate handwriting.

III

I departed this life a young man, unshriven, with all my sins upon me. I departed violently and without warning, in a distant land, on an unknown field. I was dispatched in no honourable manner, not by a soldier nor even by a rival in love, but by a witless woman, a whore in the mad king's army. I lived just long enough to witness the look of blank shock on her face, the unutterable stupidity of one who has done great evil by small design, as she dropped the loaded carbine she had been holding for her officer and watched it discharge its fatal message to my heart. I would have cried out, but I was without voice, and soon without life.

What made her drop the rifle? Was it a volley from the enemy, mustering across the field? A cannon shot? The cries of the dying?

No, I was the first to die that morning. The cannon had been silent all night, ours and theirs alike, for even the French knew better than to fire into the darkness at a foe they could not see. No, what startled my lady that morning was another whore — a cat, in fact, my lady's pampered Siamese, which jumped upon her shoulder and, suddenly unsure of its footing (but never of its welcome) dug its claws into my lady's lately caressed alabaster flesh, drawing blood as red as the poppies that stained the field before us.

My death was not recorded, either as a name on a list or as a footnote in a scholar's tome. In the space of a morning there were none to record it. For the French had taken that single shot as a challenge, to which they rose with Gallic wit, attacking in force even before the officers had taken their breakfast. There was young blood in the middle ranks, perhaps, or merely recklessness, or lust. Whatever the cause, they mounted a cavalry charge while the gunners moved up with the artillery and the infantry mustered behind.

I counted the flowering head of every poppy on the field as the horses stamped them into dust. Death did not bring sightlessness, but a clarity I had never known . . .

. . . and here came the cavalry charge, word-for-word as the little person had recited it to me the day before. It was proof of nothing, of course, except that she was capable of memorizing a couple of paragraphs of turgid prose. It was easy enough to age paper artificially, invent a seal, stamp it in wax. I knew about such things. My experience of humankind has left me in no doubt of our capacity for deception.

As quickly as they came they dispersed, and what the cavalry had begun was handily finished by the infantry. The little emperor's foot soldiers met little opposition and suffered few casualties. Within minutes our small company was annihilated. I take comfort in the knowledge that, if I was the first to die that morning, my lady soon followed. Foolishly pursuing her officer onto the field, as if she actually loved him, she was taken unaware by a French cannon ball, which separated head from belly in a most dramatic fashion. In my undiscovered state I was aware of her briefly as a fleeting, ethereal presence, the flick of a handkerchief in the corner of my eye.

Do not think I disrespected the woman's occupation. We must, each of us, make our way in the world. I am myself the whelp of a thrice-damned whore: damned by drink, disease, and dementia. The one led inexorably to the other, and I was incidental to them all. I had often wondered who my father was, a man of birth and fame or a poor wretch like herself, a tuppenny whore's unwelcome surprise. She kept me as well as she could, and gave me a sense, at least, that the world was larger than the slums of Southwark. She told me once, in a rare moment of clarity, that if you once survive the urge to die — that is, if death ever seems infinitely preferable to life, and yet you live — you are never again afraid to die. This was the greatest gift she could have given me, and I had carried it into battle many times. I had come to believe that killing was the one thing I was really good at. Now I found that I was just as good at dying. Death makes a fine teacher.

And so I found myself in a field of poppies, their blossoms strewn across the field like the blood of angels. The carnage of the day was gone. The sun shone down upon my single head, and I became aware of a vast intelligence that seemed, in turn, to be aware of me.

IV

"He saw a bright light," I said. "How surprising."

"If you had any aptitude for dating a manuscript or judging its provenance," the little person said, "you would have concluded that it was written well before the days of Dr. Elisabeth Kübler-Ross."

It was as deep an insult as I could imagine. I am a retired historian with an interest in books and manuscripts and anything else that might take me out of the sorry century I was born in. I had never heard of Elisabeth Kübler-Ross.

The little person spooned up a mouthful of soup. She had ordered the *pasta e fagioli* today, a rich potage of pancetta and cannellini beans in a tomato and chicken broth. I had stayed with the minestrone on the theory that you cannot improve on perfection.

"There wasn't a lot of clinical research into death and dying," she continued. "Theologically, on the other hand, it was quite simple: you went to heaven if you were shriven, purgatory if you weren't, and hell if you were unrepentant. There was no merciful Lord Jesus. There were terrible angels that drove you naked into the courts of time to be judged by a savage god."

"I presume your young soldier was so judged?" I opined, humouring her.

"Actually, that's the point," she said. "He wasn't."

The server brought our entrées. My steak and spaghetti didn't smell nearly as good as the little person's had the day before. Maddeningly, her pizza looked delicious. She dipped a finger into the sauce and held it to her lips. Then she asked for ketchup.

"Ketchup?" Alfredo was appalled. "I keep no ketchup in my restaurant!"

"I saw some in the kitchen when you came through," she said, then lapsed into authoritative Italian. Alfredo retreated, like a coyote from a wolf, and brought her ketchup.

"Why am I sitting here with you?" I wondered. "Why haven't I called the police? We have nothing in common, not even sanity. You are not fit to live among humans. Why don't I pick you up and throw you into the street? I may be an old man, but I can still take a rat by the scruff of its neck."

"Do you really want answers to those questions?"

"Please."

"It's because you fear ridicule. You fear being singled out. You will stare and judge, but you will not be stared at or judged. You follow the shadows, like a rat, and when the sun shines brightly on your single head, you burrow underground for fear that God might see you."

She had cut a slice of pizza into six equal portions and was shaking a dab of ketchup onto each one.

"Perhaps you should try drugs," I said. "A good anti-psychotic, even a tranquillizer, might smooth out the rough edges."

"It's not always clear," she admitted. "Sometimes it's taken a lifetime to remember, then I was taken again and had to start over. It took a few cycles to figure out that you might not always be a woman, and that was only after I'd turned up as a woman myself. It was disorienting."

"Especially such a wee one," I said. But I was on firm ground here. I had studied the various theologies of metempsychosis, I told her, "and they're all crap. Have you ever heard anyone claim he'd been lunch for cannibals in a previous life, or, to borrow your phrase, a whore in the mad king's army? True believers like to think of themselves as Joan of Arc, Catherine of Russia, Caesar Augustus, even Rasputin. They don't seem to remember the lives eked out on the streets of poisonous cities, children deliberately crippled by their beggar-master to attract the pity of passers-by, the homeless, the drones, the serial killers, the pointless lives of the ignorant and the abused — yet those are the lives that have been lived by the greater part of humankind."

"There's a difference between reincarnation and being sent back," she said, working on another slice of pizza. She stopped and looked across the table at me.

"Yes?" I prompted, for she had the aspect of one who wished to speak but was afraid to be heard. Finally, she put down her knife and fork.

"I am the prince who loved you and had to watch you banished from the court because you were base-born and unsuitable as a bride for a member of the royal family," she said. "I could have stood firm, renounced my birthright and lived in exile with the woman I loved, but I was weak, raised in luxury. I had no skills to make a life, and in the end I suppose I loved my position more than I loved you. Or perhaps I feared the loss of it more than I feared the loss of you, because I never quite believed that you would give up on me. I kept watch over you, and my agents brought daily news of your descent into gin and whoredom. I tried to intervene, but you rejected my help, again and again. You could have lived in comfort while I made a favourable marriage and produced an heir or two.

But eventually I had to face the truth: you liked it. You revelled in it, to punish me."

"That's me," I said. "Anything for a romp and a guzzle."

"But you couldn't erase my memories," she said, and smiled, and again I felt a ghostly hand caressing me, down my back, then up between my thighs. "I had seen the Promised Land."

V

She was a woman of describable beauty: dark hair pulled back from an oval face, habitually pushed behind her ears, whence it fell in curls down her neck and across her shoulders. Large mouth, voluptuous lips fallen open in repose. When she smiled, her upper lip rose to reveal the concentric white wedges of her teeth while the corners of her mouth turned down. Dark lips, dark eyes, dark brows capable of both censure and surprise. Her voice had an edge to it, not unmusical, but capable of cutting, causing pain. Her cheeks were sharply defined from the edge of her nostrils to the corners of her mouth. There was flesh on her bones, and from the way she moved her body it was evident that she had appetites and was not afraid to indulge them. She would equally arouse passion and rise to it with delight. But now she seemed to be wondering if it had been worth it, after all, as the issue of her passions — two small, beautiful, but shrilly vocal children — pawed at her upper body for comfort and attention as she attempted to communicate with her husband 100 kilometres away. It might as well have been a million. She was a lost wife in an unfamiliar town, anxious and beginning to panic as it became clear that her co-conspirator in the production of these children expected her to make the best of a bad situation. She should take shelter, he advised, before other stranded travellers took all the available rooms and left her and their children marooned in a booth in a small-town café in the middle of nowhere. Or something like it — I was only hearing her half of the conversation. Soon the roads would be impassable, but she thought he should come and get them, regardless of the risk.

"You have the four-by-four," she said into her cell phone. "It's not that far . . . I wasn't prepared for this . . . No, I can't go back to the farm, I'm halfway home already, I have the children . . . yes, but . . . damn!"

She closed her phone. "Lost the signal," she said.

I had invited the young family to share my booth, something I would never have done at Alfredo's. But this was a small-town café in the middle of nowhere and the other spaces were occupied by travellers like herself who had been advised not to travel any further. "Why didn't I take the four-by-four?"

"Because the car is more comfortable," I said.

She looked surprised, even a little frightened, then glanced out to where a dozen cars were collecting snow in the street.

"You saw us arrive," she said.

I nodded.

"I couldn't see," she said. "The wipers couldn't keep up, and the lights were useless."

"None of us is ever really prepared for the first winter storm," I reassured her, though I had prepared rather well myself, leaving the city at the last possible moment and arriving in the village at just the right time. No one knew where I was, and even if they did, there was an impenetrable wall of snow between us. Even the buses had stopped running.

"I don't know what I'm supposed to do," the young woman said.

What she meant was, she didn't know what she was supposed to feel. For she had learned something she had not known before: that the man she loved did not love her enough to risk his own life driving through a winter storm to bring her and their children safely home. It was sensible of him, no doubt, and she knew he was right, but she would remember this moment for the rest of their lives together.

"I have a room in the bed and breakfast down the street," I told her, indicating a three-storey clapboard structure that was just visible through the dirty window and the blowing snow. "You can see the sign hanging over the door, like an English pub."

"Do you think they'll have a room for us?"

"I doubt it very much," I said, "but you are welcome to mine."

"But what will you do?" she asked, with a mixture of relief for her children but rising alarm for herself. What would she be expected to do in exchange for this kindness?

I took the key from my pocket and slid it across the table. "The landlady has the only other key," I reassured her. "Her name is Meg. I've been coming here for years. Tell her I sent you."

"But who are you?"

"She'll know who I am."

Meg, too, had once been young, and impressed by such gestures. Sometimes I missed being young, but mostly I didn't. My father used to say that the chief difference between being young and being old is that it takes courage to be old, but his own father contradicted him. "The chief difference between being young and being old," said Grandfather, "is that the old are far more likely to have an extensive collection of handguns." It was with one of those guns, ironically, that my father ended his life. No loss, the world concluded. *Abiit ad plures:* he has joined the majority.

"Well, if you're sure you don't mind," she said, "I accept, with gratitude. My children accept. We'll pay you, of course. I don't have a lot of cash with me, but if you give me your name and address I'll — "

I held up a hand to silence her. "Allow an old Samaritan his gesture."

As she gathered up her children, closing coats and tying scarves, inserting small hands into woolen mittens, I went behind the café counter to make a call on the land line. A wire-haired harridan glanced up from the grill, on which various chunks of mechanically reclaimed meat were seething in grease. "You ever think of asking first, old man?"

"Piss off," I said, and made my call. I had booked a week at Meg's, with the possibility of a second. I don't like the country, but I like Meg, and for some reason her dogs — a pair of yellow Labs with more good will than sense — always greet me as a long lost friend. I had been looking forward to a few days in their company, walking through field and forest, exchanging memories as the dogs ran ahead to clear the path. The snow changed that — made it better, in fact, for now we could stay in and drink hot toddies by the fire without all that tedious exercise. Meg invited me to share her own digs, as I knew she would, but I preferred to spend the night in the café with my fellow travellers, none of whom was likely to expect more of me than I could provide.

"What should I say to her?" asked the young mother as she herded her children to the door.

"She's expecting you," I replied.

I watched them through the window as they turned to shadows in the falling snow: a triangle of love, the woman reaching her hands down to the extent of her body and her children reaching up to the extent of theirs: four short legs kicking snow, two long and lovely legs keeping patient pace. If I had ever required payment from her, that was enough.

I had the harridan make me some soup, which she poured from a can and served with two slim salted crackers wrapped in cellophane. As food it was unacceptable, but we had come to an understanding over the years: I ate what she prepared, and was grateful if she remembered to put her teeth in when she served it.

"How's the soup?" she asked.

"You could cure fish in it," I replied.

An RCMP constable came in, stamping his boots and brushing snow from his cap and shoulders. He announced that the highway had been closed. There was an immediate uproar.

"But I have to be — "

"My family is expecting — "

"I have an appointment at — "

"Travel is prohibited," the constable said, in a tone that conveyed both sympathy and authority.

"Can you do that?" someone demanded.

"We're as stranded as you are." The constable waved a hand at the weather beyond the window. "My partner is doing one last circuit of the town to look for stragglers, but after that we'll be joining you here."

"What am I supposed to do?" demanded the harridan.

"Count your blessings," said the constable. "These people are staying until the roads are passable, and I imagine most of them will want something to eat sooner or later."

It was going to be a long evening, and a longer night. People made themselves as comfortable as they could, some bringing in blankets and food from their cars, others ordering items from the laminated menus on the counter. The other officer arrived, fog lights barely visible in the blowing snow and the gathering darkness. Coffee was brewed, potatoes fried, buns toasted, burgers turned. Every so often the harridan nipped into the back for a smoke. It was where she lived, so it technically did not fall under the draconian purview of the tobacco Nazis. Whatever her complaints, it was going to be a profitable night for her.

VI

There was a rich and rancid stench from the vomitorium as Marcus staggered out.

"In the name of Macha, close the door!" the woman shouted.

Marcus paused, attempted briefly to find hand-holds on the nearest wall, failed, and sank slowly to his knees.

"Who speaks?" he demanded, searching the dimness with eyes that would not focus.

"Macha, the crow goddess!"

He peered dimly in the direction of the voice. "You are no Roman," he said.

"Nor was I meant to be," she replied.

"Who are you then? Who speaks to me from the darkness?"

"I have told you. I am fierce Macha, who delights to dance among the slain."

And indeed, she might have been, except that she lay in my arms, and I knew her. She was naked and voluptuous, a whore in the mad king's army. I had loved her and lost, and loved again and lost again, and here I was again, loving and despising in the same breath as she lay in my arms, my heartache . . .

VII

"Are you with us, old man?" A stranger was shaking me by the shoulder. "Are you with us?" he repeated, louder.

I wanted to tell him there was no reason to shout, but one of the RCMP officers was roughly exploring my mouth with his fingers.

"Are these you own teeth?" he asked, trying unsuccessfully to pull them out.

"Whose did you think they were?" I demanded, when I was able to speak.

"When someone's having a stroke," the officer said, defensively, "it's important to remove their teeth."

"I'm not having a stroke," I said, taking a napkin from the table and wiping the dirt and gun-metal of the officer's fingers from my lips. "I fell asleep. I had a dream. I don't think *she* wrote it. She couldn't have. I was in Roman Britain and Marcus was coming out of the vomitorium."

"His mind is wandering," said one of the officers.

"His mind is always wandering," said the harridan.

"Only because you're so boring," I started to say, but even as I spoke I felt a weird vibration start up in my chest, as if a guitarist had begun playing a rapid dance. The guitarist was soon joined by a drummer and a bass player. Then a tap dancer moved in and tried to take over the whole production. The drummer was having none of that. Neither was the guitarist. They both renewed their efforts. Then someone started playing the bagpipes in the background.

"He really is having a stroke now," said someone.

"Call 911."

"And say what?" asked someone else. "Come out and die with us?"

A child wailed in fright.

"Nobody's going to die," a mother soothed.

I was aware of careful hands opening my jacket and vest, loosening my tie, emptying my pockets. The officers examined the items they had taken from my pockets.

"Forty-five dollars and change," said one. "House keys, car keys."

"And two dollars in Canadian Tire money," said the other.

"Do you think he knows it isn't real?"

"Get him up on the counter," said a familiar voice.

"You know him?"

"He's having a heart attack," said the little person. "He's *always* having a heart attack. Get him up on the counter."

"Where did you come from?" asked one of the officers.

"We don't have much time," she said, exasperated. "Get him up on the counter or I shall have to hurt you."

The harridan swept the counter clean with a forearm, scattering condiments and laminated menus. The two RCMP officers lifted me onto the counter, where the little person straddled my torso and started performing CPR.

"Not this time, you bastard," I heard her mutter as she tilted my head back to open the airway, then loudly in my ear: "Are you still in there, old man?" She waited a moment, her ear to my mouth. Getting no response, she grasped my shoulders and shook them. "Not this time, you bastard!" she repeated, and she clasped her hands, one on top of the other over my breast bone and began performing chest compressions to kick-start my heart. I could have told her she was wasting her time. I wasn't coming back.

VIII

During the war they made love exhaustively, almost desperately. Each night they redefined the term. It would start with a look, a gesture, and without speaking they each knew what the other wanted, and, if it were possible, wanted it more. It rose in them like a fever, until it was the only thing that mattered, until it raged, until they could not imagine they had ever felt anything else. When their bodies met it was with the passion of a prophecy fulfilled, and their nakedness was a talisman engraven with the magic virtues and the secret meaning of things, and he thought that if he could hold on one more minute, one more second, if he could withhold himself long enough to hold her a little more tightly and enter her a little more deeply, their bodies might fuse, and their minds, and then sexless in that dark place where sex is master he might chance upon the essential truth, the meaning of the farce, as a man who has wandered long in the desert might see Christ in a drop of water. But it was over so quickly, the body spends itself so quickly, and afterward they made the bed like tame domestic creatures, each casting furtive glances past the other, as if the master might suddenly appear and put them out.

IX

I remembered watching a bullfight in Spain: a magnificent animal tormented to madness, its confusion giving way first to fear and then to rage, and then to a numb acceptance of its fate as its human tormentors danced around it on horseback. I watched the bull toss its head, watched the red blood spout from its nostrils in a flying arc over its back and then forward onto the sand. The creature fell to its knees, aware of nothing now but the fighter with his cape and the empty hand that had held the sword. It dipped its head, almost in obeisance, and permitted itself to die. As the matador bowed to the cheering crowd and the body of the bull was dragged away, I thought, *You people have no idea who really won this contest.*

But I had never been to Spain.

"I see you are remembering," said a voice nearby.

I could sense by odour and feel that I was in a hospital bed: the crisp linen, the scent of antiseptic, and beneath that, barely perceptible, the constant companion of illness: fear. I would not open my eyes. I had no wish to look upon the world I thought I had finally left. But the little person was reading to me beside the bed, and I couldn't close my ears. I could hear the pages shuffling in her hands.

X

If we are to believe the studies of social scientists and medical researchers, men think about sex every two or three minutes from puberty to the grave. Building a career or a stock portfolio, acquiring the material goods that mark our progress in the world, are potent but essentially transitory distractions from the biological imperative that rules us.

The same studies tell us what we would have learned from experience in any case: women don't feel the same way. It is no coincidence that the predominant strain of pornography, from de Sade's erotic humiliations to the wholesale degradations of body and beast on the Internet, panders to the illusion that they do. Woman as predator — women behaving like men — is the ruling philosophy of a multi-billion-dollar industry that is based, in the final analysis, on the myth that women want sex as much as men, if not more. Dr. Johnson would have called it the triumph of hope over experience.

Sex comes up in conversation less frequently but with more humour as we age. Twice in my 40s I had occasion to remark, quite casually, on the frequency of sexual intercourse among newlyweds of my generation, or even newly-mets, for those were liberal times. In my own experience, once a day did not seem excessive, twice a day was the norm, and three times in a day seemed hardly immoderate for a healthy young couple falling in love.

"Just a minute," said one friend, eyes wide "Do you mean once a day, as in every day?"

"It diminishes after a year or two," I said.

I could see him working out the opportunities he had missed. "Marilyn!" I imagined him shouting from the doorway as he arrived home that night. "Rob says once a day is minimum! Twice a day is normal!"

Another friend, a classical scholar well-versed in the Hebrew scriptures, shook his head in admiration and despair and said, "Robert, you have seen the Promised Land."

XI

It made a certain sense. That was my name, after all. Robert. Finally, I allowed my eyes to open. "Did you write that?"

"No, you did," she said.

"So you were the whore in the mad king's army."

"I was a soldier in Wellesley's army," she corrected me. "You were the whore that killed me. We were together in Roman Britain, Georgian England, Spain, Canada, wherever you can imagine. It doesn't matter. The only thing that matters is that I've got you here, alive, at the end of another life. But this time we're both alive, and you can't run from me any more."

"Tell me why I should believe you."

"Because this is the first opportunity I've had to tell you the truth."

"Oh yes?" I said. "And what is the truth?"

"I'm sorry."

"You're sorry? For what?"

"For killing you. For pursuing you. For seducing you. For abandoning you. For using you. And for being killed, pursued, seduced, used, and abandoned in turn. I'm sorry."

"Is that all?"

"It's less than all," she said, placing her small hands in mine, "but it's more than everything."

I felt her soft, dry skin, warm as the sun.

"We can go now," she said.

"Can we, really?"

She nodded and smiled, and in her smile I suddenly knew her, knew him, I knew the ones I had loved and killed.

"Thank you," I said, amazed.

Epilogue

Seven o'clock on a Wednesday evening. A sky of bruised pearl. Light shimmered on the water as the sun followed its long arc to the west. It would rain later as the thunderheads moved in, but for now I was sitting on the deck, enjoying a glass of wine and thinking about the sirloin steak that was awaiting me in the cabin. I was reading *The Fifth Woman* by the Swedish author Henning Mankell. I had finished the intriguing prologue and was moving on to chapter one, where the old man had just finished writing a poem about a woodpecker, when the chair collapsed beneath me — or rather, behind me. My skull cracked against the wall of the cabin. My body jackknifed, knees to chin. I lost consciousness for an instant, but when I came to I was still holding the book in one hand, my glass of wine in the other. Getting up was not an option. I considered my situation. *How easily we are reduced to helplessness*, I thought. *And death.* I imagined someone finding me curled up and abandoned, the crows eating my eyeballs. I struggled to free myself, but I was wedged between the seat of the chair and the wall of the cabin. A small aircraft flew overhead, coming in low beneath the clouds. There was a puddle of water on the deck from the previous rainfall. As I craned my neck to watch the plane, my body rolled sideways. I felt the cold water seeping through my jeans. I drew my elbows up and slowly raised myself to my knees. My head ached, but I didn't spill a drop. I examined the chair, saw where it had failed. I resisted the temptation to toss it into the forest. I examined the other chairs, stacked against the railing of the deck. They were all broken in the same place. A manufacturer's defect. *None of the chairs on the deck is safe*, I thought. Then the world collapsed around me.

Wakaw is a crooked lake, a widening of a minor river in an erratic valley carved out by a retreating glacier. Not much happens there, unless the pilot of a single-engine Cessna decides one Wednesday evening in August to drop the body of a woman where you happen to be disentangling yourself from a broken chair on the deck of your summer home. She took out the west railing and a portion of the decking before coming to rest on the forest floor ten feet below.

I looked up to watch the Cessna disappearing over the tree line. I heard a motorboat on the lake. I saw the squat figure of Victor Kott, perched like a daub of toothpaste in the rear of his fourteen-foot Alumacraft. I waved him in, trying to impart a sense of urgency with my arms. If Victor saw me, he gave no sign. Fifteen minutes later I heard the creaking of ungreased oarlocks as he came back into sight, rowing close to shore, cursing.

"Engine broke down," he yelled over the water. "Damn thing just —"

"I could use some help here, Victor."

I was a dozen feet back from the shore, knee-high in underbrush. I realized he probably couldn't see the body from the lake. She had been a pretty woman, her face miraculously unmarked by the fall and whatever had happened before that. She was wearing a white blouse and a grey skirt: office clothes, conservative. Understandably shoeless. She had come to rest on her right side, facing away from the lake, one arm beneath her and the other thrown out as if to break her fall. She was blonde and pale, without makeup, but there

• Epilogue •

was on her face no ante-mortem rictus of pain or fear. She looked as if she had died in peace.

Victor was easing the boat in to shore, gazing up at the ruins of my deck. "Jesus, Molloy, what have you been drinking?" Then he saw the corpse.

"Guy probably meant to drop her in the water," I conjectured, "but it's a narrow lake."

"Guy?" he asked. "What guy?"

"The guy in the plane." I gestured upward, then realized that if Victor hadn't been looking, he wouldn't have seen the plane, and he certainly wouldn't have heard it over the drone of his ancient Evinrude.

"A plane went over," I explained. "A Cessna 172. She" — I indicated the corpse — "either jumped or was pushed from it."

Victor looked around, as if he were seeking a better explanation, or perhaps a means of escape. "How'd you know it was a Cessna?"

"High wing design, non-retractable landing gear. It's the most common aircraft on earth. What does it matter?"

"You should call 911."

"I don't have a phone."

"What do you mean, you don't have a phone?"

"I mean I don't have a phone." Victor liked to hear things twice. "I don't come here to talk. I come here to read books and drink wine and eat steak. For the love of mercy, Victor, a woman just dropped out of the sky. Do you think if I had a phone I wouldn't have called someone by now?"

He fished beneath his lifejacket and produced a shiny new BlackBerry. There was a tower just across the lake, so there was little chance that there would be no reception. He checked the horizon just in case. His hands were shaking as he punched in the digits.

There was a clap of thunder, and it started to rain.

A farmer south of Wakaw later described the scene to me: the plane stalling in mid-air, the slow turn, the first spin, then the precipitous fall to earth. He seemed a bit disappointed that it hadn't erupted in a ball of fire.

"The fuel tanks on a Cessna 172 are in the wings," I explained to him. "They won't burst into flame unless they rupture, and then you need a spark to ignite the fumes."

"She just hammered in," said the farmer, ascribing the usual gender to the plane.

The RCMP were interested in my knowledge of the aircraft.

"Did you know it was going to stall?" they asked.

"I didn't know it *had* stalled until you guys told me you were attending a plane crash and that's why you were late getting to the body below my cabin."

"How did you know it was the same plane?"

"It was the only one I saw."

Victor was no help. He had seen nothing, heard nothing. He had no reason to believe that I had not slaughtered the woman myself and thrown her off my deck, taking out the west railing and a portion of the decking in the process. I thought this was a bit much, under the circumstances. I had barely escaped with my own life tonight, after the chair collapsed, and I still hadn't had my steak. My hands were shaking, and I was shivering from the cold.

"Let's take it from the beginning, Mr. Molloy."

"The Cessna 172 seats four," I said, "and it's easy to fly. The 152 looks the same but it's smaller, and the doors have been known to pop open in turbulence or during a rough landing. That's never been a problem with the 172. The door handle lies flush with the arm rest, and you open it by pulling the handle all the way rearward. Whoever opened the door of that plane did it on purpose. But he had to slow down as much as possible to reduce the air flow,

• Epilogue •

otherwise he couldn't have opened the door wide enough to push the woman out. My guess is, his arms weren't strong enough and he had to do it with his feet. By the time he'd maneuvered himself back into his seat and heard the stall warning, he'd lost control of the aircraft and didn't have the altitude to recover."

"Sounds as if you planned it yourself," said Victor, who was dripping wet and in an extremely bad mood. We were all dripping wet. The rain hadn't stopped and the woman's body was still lying in the brush below my deck, periodically illuminated by flashes of lightning. One RCMP officer was outside keeping an eye on her while the other dripped on my kitchen floor and asked questions. There were two more at the crash site. The pilot had been pronounced dead at the scene, they told us. He had been wearing a dark blue suit.

"Are you a pilot yourself, Mr. Molloy?"

"Are you kidding? You wouldn't get me up in one of those things. They're death traps."

"Then how do you know so much about them?"

"I wrote a book about single-engine aircraft for a private flying club in Calgary. Many of the members flew Cessnas."

"How can you write a book about planes if you refuse to fly in them?"

"Good Lord, you don't have to know anything to write a book. You just have to sound believable."

"Can I go now?" It was Victor, shivering in his golf shirt.

"We'd rather you wait until the forensics team arrives."

"What, all the way from Saskatoon? What do they hope to discover, that a woman fell from an airplane onto Molloy's deck? I think we already know that."

"We'd rather you waited," the officer repeated.

"How were you planning to get home, Victor?" I asked. "Through the woods in the rain or down the lake in your broken-down boat? Of course, out on the lake there's a better chance of being struck by lightning."

"Next time I'm just going to row right by," he said.

The second officer came inside. "Your turn," he said, water dripping from his uniform cap and flowing off his rain cloak. It would have been churlish to complain. I understood that it was necessary to secure the scene from intruders, including wildlife, though what the forensics team intended to do when they got here was anybody's guess. It's not as if my deck was a crime scene. The crime, if any, had been committed hundreds of metres in the air above.

"How about some tea?" I said. "Would anybody like some tea?"

"I would like fourteen ounces of scotch," said Victor.

I gave him one to start with, and I took a pain killer. My head was throbbing where it had hit the cabin wall, and I was feeling light-headed.

"Might be an idea to call your wife," I suggested.

He went pale. "She must think I've drowned in the storm."

"Good luck explaining what really happened," I said.

He went into the next room with his BlackBerry. A minute later I heard him saying, "It's not my fault, Pauline. It's not my fault."

"At least he didn't say it was my fault," I said.

"Wonder why Pauline didn't try to call *him*," the constable remarked.

"She saw my iPhone beside the land line and thought it would be pointless," Victor explained, returning to the kitchen.

"She doesn't know you bought a BlackBerry?" I asked.

"She does now," he said, and helped himself to more scotch.

I took pity on them and handed out beach towels. They were new. I'd bought them for myself and I'd been looking forward to using each one, in turn, because there is nothing so comforting as

• Epilogue •

a fresh towel when you've just come out of the lake, and they were never the same after being washed in the local water.

There were shots fired. The constable drew his Smith and Wesson and called out over the deck, "You all right, Vern?"

"Wolf!" Vern shouted back. "There's a goddamn wolf out here!"

"There are no wolves around here," said Victor.

"There's a pregnant bitch denning in the forest up the hill," I said.

"Probably looking for a sheltered place to whelp," said the constable, holstering his sidearm.

"I didn't know that," said Victor, and his whole concept of going home changed. "I'll have to stay till the forensics team arrives, of course, I see that now, I'm a witness and — "

"You're not a witness," said the constable. "Who told you you were a witness? Vern?"

Victor nodded.

"Vern likes to go by the book, even when he hasn't read it," said the constable. "We've got your name and number. Or one of them, anyway. You can leave any time you want."

"No, I think Vern was right. Don't you think so, James?"

He so rarely called me by my first name that I didn't know who he was talking to for a moment, but then I said yes, he should stay, and he should build a fire, too, because August nights can be cold by the lake, and he should put the kettle on, and if he wanted to get out of his wet clothes there was one of my late father's bathrobes in the far bedroom that would probably fit him. It didn't, as it happened, and he bulged hairily above the waist. He draped his wet clothes over the backs of my dining room chairs, where they hung like limp, dead things. He wore plaid boxer shorts. I dried myself and changed into my own bathrobe and began to feel warm for the first time since my chair collapsed. We soon had quite the little domestic scene happening. Vern came in from outside for a cup of tea and never went back out, for he had no more desire to be eaten by a wolf in the dark than Victor did. When the forensics team finally called from the top of the hill — my cabin is halfway down the south bank of the lake and not visible from the road — Vern went up to direct them down while the other constable took up his post by the body. It was twelve o'clock and the rain had stopped, but you could still hear distant thunder.

There were three of them, two men and an efficient-looking young woman with a ponytail tucked into her cap. They looked like children to me, they were so young, but they moved like clockwork, speaking in verbal shorthand, each aware of his or her function and highly skilled in the execution of it. With Vern and the other constable's help, they set up floodlights and took photographs, then they removed the body in a two-person sling, as if they had done it a hundred times before, one officer following another up the steep path to the road. They taped off a section of brush and forest around where the woman had landed, and said they would be back in daylight for a more thorough examination of the area.

It was three AM when I finally put my steak on the grill, along with one for Victor. He had finished the bottle of scotch. At 3:15 we dined on sirloin and Caesar salad, with a nice Merlot.

"Poor woman," said Victor.

"It was almost as if they were handling a doll," I said.

"Who?"

"The forensics team. The way they acted, you'd think it was a rag doll that fell out of the sky, not a human woman."

"I suppose you get used to it."

"I don't see how."

"Pauline didn't believe me."

"She'll have to tomorrow."

"Do you really think he pushed her?"

• EPILOGUE •

"I don't know what to think, Victor. This has never happened before."

"I think I'm in shock, a little — like it's been creeping up on me."

"Keep yourself warm and try to get some sleep."

We fell into bed shortly before four — he in my parents' old bedroom, which I entered only to dust once a month or so, and I in mine. But I couldn't sleep for wondering what had happened to the old man who wrote the poem about the woodpecker. I went out to the kitchen where I had left *The Fifth Woman* open to dry. The book was still sodden from the rain, but readable by my bedside lamp. I learned something about migrating wildfowl, then I was appalled to find the old man impaled on sharpened bamboo poles. *Revenge for something*, I thought. I checked the ending and saw that I had 409 pages to go, so at least I'd have something to distract me tomorrow.

Victor's golf shirt and chinos had shrunk, and seemed to impede his breathing. I listened to his flip-flops flip-flopping down the stairs to the beach. He left after baling out his boat, which had taken on a lot of rain during the night. I heard the oars creaking in their locks long after I thought he should have reached home. I took another pain killer because my head still ached. I stripped Victor's bed and put the sheets in the laundry. It would be the first time they had been washed in ten years. I went to the edge of the broken deck and briefly surveyed the ground below. There was nothing in the depression in the undergrowth to suggest a human shape, let alone a female one. In a week there would be no sign at all. The forest takes over everything. I drove into town to buy another bottle of scotch.

The forensics team arrived much later than I had expected, having driven back to Saskatoon the night before to deliver the well-dressed corpses to a pathologist and then come back to examine the crash site with investigators from the Transportation

Safety Board. They refused my offer of coffee and set to work immediately, combing the ground, retrieving shreds of fabric hanging on saskatoon berry bushes. I doubt they expected to find much, for it was obvious what had happened: a woman fell out of the sky and was killed on impact with my deck. Then the female investigator found something unexpected. "It's human," she said, and started to dig. Within an hour they had retrieved enough of a female skeleton to draw some unflattering conclusions about my family, who had owned the property since 1952.

At the end of August Victor and Pauline pulled up their boat and packed up their belongings and moved back to the city for the winter. They were both school teachers and had to re-engage with reality in September, when they would be known once again as Mr. Kott and Ms Bramwell-Kott. Normally I would have followed, but I was rebuilding the deck and was loath to leave until I had finished. I had once written a book entitled *Fifteen Outdoor Summer Projects for the Do-It-Yourselfer*, and I felt fairly confident that I knew what I was doing.

In September the lake turned cold and calm. The Canada geese gathered in their thousands, with ducks of every stripe, mallards and mud hens. They would stay as long as there was open water. The snow geese were not so brave. I watched them flying south in the night in their undisciplined rows, white chuckling birds reflecting the moonlight on their wings. The trees turned yellow, the birch and poplar, and the unpicked saskatoon berries withered on the stem.

I finished *The Fifth Woman*, a dark tale of revenge, as well as *The Return of the Dancing Master*, a darker tale of Nazism and revenge, also by Henning Mankell. Now I was reading Stieg Larsson's trilogy, starting with *The Girl with the Dragon Tattoo*. It, too, had a Nazi subtext, and I was sure I would find revenge eventually.

• Epilogue •

I seemed no longer able to function without Swedish literature.

The most dramatic events of August had turned out to have a fairly simple explanation. The post-mortem examination of the woman who had fallen from the sky revealed ante-mortem bruising on her upper left arm and thigh, including the imprint of a heel matching the shoe the pilot was found wearing at the crash site. This confirmed my original hypothesis: that he had pushed her from the aircraft with his feet. An examination of the Cessna uncovered no mechanical or electronic malfunctions, leading investigators once again to my original hypothesis: the plane had slowed to stalling speed and there wasn't sufficient altitude to recover, so "she just hammered in," as the farmer had so eloquently described it. The pilot was killed on impact. There was some question as to whether his widow would receive his life insurance, for the company tried to make the case that it had been a suicide pact. The man and the woman had been known to be having an affair — "an office romance," according to the local paper, "a hopeless affair of the heart" — and it is well known that insurance companies don't pay off in the event of suicide. But suicide could not be proved, and there was no clause in the policy preventing the wife of a murderer from collecting her husband's insurance.

There was no doubt the man was a murderer. There was no doubt the woman had been alive when he pushed her from the plane. The fact that she was heavily drugged at the time and could not have known what was happening did not diminish his guilt. The drug used was odd, though: Zopiclone, a non-benzodiazepine hypnotic used in the treatment of insomnia. Though a controlled substance, it was not considered dangerous or addictive, and physicians had been prescribing it for years as a treatment for sleep disorders. Death is the ultimate treatment for a sleep disorder.

The insurance company thought it was on firmer ground in refusing to pay out the woman's insurance. The victim, a single mother of two, had clearly intended to commit suicide, they argued, or she would not have taken an overdose. The fact that she had been killed by someone else before her own aim could be accomplished did not lessen her guilt or alter her intention. The fact that suicide by Zopiclone was virtually unknown did not affect the insurance company's argument.

I was able to follow the case on the Internet because I had a telephone installed at the cabin. Bringing the modern world into my sanctuary was not as traumatic as I had feared: I could still read and drink wine and eat steak, and I didn't have to answer the phone if I didn't want to. The dial-up modem was as slow as a glacier, but I was in no hurry.

I said it was a fairly simple explanation, but nothing human is simple. The legal bickering would work its way through the courts, but the whole of the mystery would never be solved. What had the couple planned to do when they went aloft in a rented Cessna and headed under the thunder clouds toward Wakaw Lake? Had the pilot intended to drop the woman in the water? Had she asked to be dropped there? Did she take the Zopiclone before they took off or did she wait until they were in the air? She must have been relatively unimpaired to get into the plane. Did she use Zopiclone because it was the only thing she had, or had it been supplied by her partner? Why were they so well dressed, he in a business suit and she in a skirt and blouse?

By a startling coincidence, her surname was the same as mine: Molloy. Mary Molloy. She was no relation, that I knew of, but I couldn't help but wonder if this was no coincidence at all. Had she been sent to me in this tragically preposterous manner to fulfill some other purpose — sent by a God with a peculiarly warped sense of humour?

Unlike Mary Molloy, the woman whose skeleton was unearthed by forensic investigators below my deck was nameless and without

• Epilogue •

mourners. Suspicion fell upon me only briefly, for it was apparent after the first, cursory examination that the remains, although of a young woman, were older than I, maybe as old as the bison skull that had washed up on the shore one spring when I was a child. Roots had grown down among her ribs, and the bones were discoloured from the iron in the soil. My father and mother had first come here in 1952, but the woman had been in the ground long before they thought of conceiving me in the far bedroom. The bones had been revealed by time and erosion, and by the curious happenstance of another woman falling out of the sky. The skeleton was small, but mature. She would have been shorter than many of her contemporaries. The cranial index, the facial profile, the complex suture patterns, and the zygomatic arches on her skull indicated that she was Aboriginal, possibly Cree. So she, too, had called the lake *wakaw*, crooked.

What had she been doing here? She would not have been collecting water, for the lake water is highly laxative, owing to a profusion of natural salts. She might have been fishing, for at one time perch and pickerel were plentiful. She might have been washing herself when someone — a coward — crept up from behind and struck her in the back of the head. She may have suffered as she died, unlike Mary Molloy. She may have struggled against the darkness. All that is certain is that she died by violence, and her murderer put her in a shallow grave to hide his crime.

All my life I had thought of this place as home, as sanctuary, as a safe retreat when the world came clamouring at the door, and all the while I was living on top of a murdered woman's body. They took her bones away, I don't know where. It sounds preposterous, but I missed her. I thought she should have been allowed to stay where she had died — where she had rested, perhaps, in the end.

In October the landscape became inexpressibly sad. Here was everything, I thought, and here was nothing. Here was earth, sky, and water. It contained all things, yet it was utterly empty.

I moved my books and desk into my parents' old room and gave their bed to the Good Neighbour Store in town. That, too, was not as traumatic as I had feared.

A deep stillness settled over the earth as the humans left and the water froze. Each morning the ice had moved out a little further from the shore. The air took on a purity it hadn't had before. The light was clearer. In November the snow came. The stubborn geese had stayed until the last moment. On the first morning the lake was frozen from shore to shore I heard the last of them leaving, high above where the Cessna had flown three months before.

I brought out my winter wardrobe and closed up my condo in the city. My agent was appalled until she discovered that she could deal with me just as effectively in one place as another, and my literary output, if you could call it that, was not the sort that required frequent appearances on radio or television. I read fiction as I waited for web pages to load. I chopped birch for the stove. The occasional plane flew overhead, and once or twice I saw the wolf close by, smiling, mistress of all she surveyed.

In the local branch of the regional library I found a novel by Henning Mankell, *Italian Shoes*. "It seems not so long ago since I was in the first act," I read. "Now the epilogue has already started."

Every day I went out onto my newly rebuilt deck and leaned over the empty grave with a glass of wine. I spilled a few drops into the undergrowth, as an offering to the soul of the woman who had lain there for so long. It became a ritual. I spoke to her sometimes, telling her how a woman had fallen out of the sky to disturb her grave. I apologized for what had happened to her.

"You watched over me all my life," I said. "I can keep vigil for a winter."

ENVIRONMENTAL BENEFITS STATEMENT

Thistledown Press saved the following resources by printing the pages of this book on chlorine free paper made with 100% post-consumer waste.

TREES	WATER	ENERGY	SOLID WASTE	GREENHOUSE GASES
7 FULLY GROWN	3,080 GALLONS	2 MILLION BTUs	196 POUNDS	683 POUNDS

 Environmental impact estimates were made using the Environmental Paper Network Paper Calculator. For more information visit www.papercalculator.org.